U0001052

喚醒你的英文語感！

Get a Feel for English !

喚醒你的英文語感！

Get a Feel for English !

愈忙愈要學英文

大家**開會**說英文

風行**500**大企業的*Leximodel*字串學習法

BIZ ENGLISH
for
BUSY PEOPLE

現今開會不僅止於面對面的會議，
視訊和電話會議
儼然是未來趨勢之一，
只要熟悉本書彙整出的高頻、速效字串，
大會議達人技巧和 26 類會議必備語庫，
生意商機和自信魅力扶搖直上！
會議英語超流利，互動能量無可擋！

附1片實戰
MP3

貝塔語言出版
Beta Multimedia Publishing

作者◎商英教父 Quentin Brand

Contents 目錄

Unit 1 ▷ 有效會議的重要事項

Unit 2 ▷ 展開會議

Unit 3 ▶ 資訊交流型會議：處理資訊

Unit 4 ▶ 問題解決型會議：處理問題

Contents

The Leximodel

▶ 引言與學習目標

電話會議其實是，會議的參與者可能無法面對面親身和對方會晤的會議。就用語和目的層面來說，親臨現場的會議與以電話進行的會議，兩者相似度很高，均含有主導人、會議目的以及議程等三項成分，而且若事先未經規畫或事後未加追蹤，則兩者可能都將徒勞無功。

近幾年來在跨國委外和全球化的發展趨勢之下，世界已經逐漸走向扁平化。許多行業中的工作團隊彼此可能相隔千里之遙，所以通訊會議便成了這些團隊保持密切、密集商業溝通的常用管道。除此之外，加上油價昂貴，搭乘飛機的旅費及時間成本節節升高，還有恐怖主義與全球傳染病的威脅，為公事出差的作法已逐年減少，反而常有公司砸錢投資電子會議設備，並訓練員工操作這些設備。在幾年前台灣和中國南部爆發 SARS 疫情時，這種商業作法的新趨勢尤為明顯，自此之後更逐漸演變為常態了。未來這波新興的開會趨勢極可能會持續增長，很快便將成為商務人士履歷表上必備的工作技能之一。

對許多英文非母語的人士來說，以英文開會可說是一項語文能力的全新挑戰。以英語進行面對面協商溝通的會議時，常會遇到聽不懂對方的口音、溝通破裂、簡報要求清楚明快、迅速達成決議、處理意見相左等狀況，若發生在看不到其他發言人的會議中，這些都會是更加棘手的難題。關於「對方聽懂了嗎？」、「想表達什麼意思？」等疑問，都得從對方的微笑、皺眉等視覺上的線索加以了解，但在電話會議時卻無從得知，因此，我們只得更加倚重聽力來加以判斷。拜科技之賜，讓我們能夠即時與世界各個角落的人取得聯繫，這項進步簡直就如同奇蹟一般地不可思議，但科技本身並非完美無缺，不時仍會發生通訊遲緩、回音干擾以及通話品質不良等情況。

本書旨在幫助中文人士在以英文開會時能夠得心應手，並且經由本書所提供的必備語彙和練習，練就出效率有加的開會本領，進而增進以英文進行電話會議時的自信。同時，本書所提供語庫和技巧練習，在親臨現場的傳統會議中也都派得上用場。

現在請先花一點時間閱讀下面的問題，並寫下答案。於作答時，請先暫時別往下閱讀，待作答完畢再繼續閱讀。

Task　1

請思考以下問題，寫下自己的答案。

● 你購買本書的原因為何？

● 你希望從本書學到什麼？

● 你以英文開電話會議和一般會議時，會遇到哪些問題？

從以下針對上述問題所提出的答案選項，勾選出最貼近自己想法的答案。

1. 你購買本書的原因為何？

☐ 我買這本書是想找到一個學習英文的方法，來滿足我專業上的需求。

☐ 我真的忙得不得了。我不想浪費時間去學工作上用不到的東西，或是練習在職場中派不上用場的語言。

☐ 我看到這本書的封面上寫著「大家開會說英文」。因為我們開會都是用英文，我覺得我的表現還可以再好一點。電話會議對我尤其困難，在根本看不到人的情況下，單憑紛雜的口音進行判別，在這方面我有待加強。

☐ 我希望這本書可以引導我多做練習，同時提供一些簡單明瞭的參考重點，形式上類似英文辭典，但卻是專門針對英文電話會議和一般會議設計的，讓我可以隨身攜帶和查閱。

☐ 我需要一本了解我有哪些專業需求的書！

2. 你希望從本書學到什麼？

☐ 我想學最需要用到的字彙和文法，來處理我的商業事務。

☐ 我想學會如何更有效地進行電話會議和一般會議。

☐ 我希望這本書能指出我用法上的錯誤，並加以糾正，同時更希望這本書就像是我的私人語言家教。

☐ 我想學的是可以通行國際的英文。我的客戶有的是英國人、有的是美國人，甚至在歐洲、印度和東南亞也都有我的客戶。所以我希望世界各地的客戶都聽得懂我的英文。

☐ 我覺得我在一般會議和正式會議中的發言，肯定相當枯燥乏味。因為我講話太慢，對自己的英文發音也不甚有信心。

☐ 我英文念得不太好，也很討厭文法。我覺得文法很無趣，而且比和一大群老外在電話上開會還要可怕！！可是我也知道，文法非懂不可。所以我希望能加強英文卻不需死背文法。

❑ 我想找到自學就可以改善英文的方法。我工作上常需要用到英語，但我知道自己並沒有善用這項環境優勢來培養專業的英文能力。所以我希望這本書能教我如何做到這一點。

3. 你以英文開電話會議和一般會議時，會遇到哪些問題？

❑ 我最大的問題在於缺乏自信。一對一的時候沒問題，但要面對一大堆以英文為母語的人或其他外國人時，我就會變得異常緊張，尤其是在看不到對方的情況，譬如電話會議。

❑ 如果對方講什麼我都聽不懂，可不可以請他們再講一遍？我不想讓人家覺得很煩，但清楚理解對方的訊息卻又很重要。所以想知道請對方解釋清楚、又不致失禮的方法。

❑ 我發現有時候人家會誤解我的話。我不知道是我講得不清楚，還是他們自己沒聽懂，總之我都得加以解釋或更正對方，同時又得顧及禮貌。真不知該怎麼辦？

❑ 我覺得有時候很難表達自己的想法，因為沒有適當的辭彙可以運用。

❑ 我最大的問題在於聽力。我不僅需要和印度、新加坡或美國等英語人士聯繫，和其他如日本人和法國人等非英語人士也有商業往來。所以，有時候會由於發音的不同而產生溝通上的問題。

❑ 我想要提高開會的效率。有時候我覺得參加會議根本是在浪費時間，因為沒有人持續追蹤之前會議中討論過的事項。

❑ 因為我是工作小組的組長，有時候難免會需要主持一些例行性或正式的會議。但我對主持會議不是很在行，尤其是以英文開會的時候。

❑ 我常常連該說些什麼都不知所措！

❑ 我希望對英文的掌握度就像對中文的一樣，但是我知道我的英文不夠靈光，用英文思考快不起來。

你可能同意以上這幾點的部分或全部，你也可能有其他我沒有想到的答案。不過先容我自我介紹。

我是 Quentin Brand，我教了十七年的英文，對象包括來自世界各地像各位這樣的商界專業人士，而且我有好幾年的時間都待在台灣。客戶包括企業各個階層的人，從大型跨國企業國外分公司的經理，到擁有海外市場的小型本地公司所雇用的基層實習生不等。我教過初學者，也教過英文程度非常高的人，他們都曾經表達過上述的心聲。他們想的事和各位一樣，就是想找到一種簡單實用的方法學習英文。

各位，你們已經找到了！這些年來，我開發了一套教導和學習英文的方法，專門幫各位這樣忙碌的商界人士解決疑慮。這套辦法的核心概念稱作 Leximodel，是一種以嶄新的角度看待英語的教學法。目前 Leximodel 已經獲得全世界一些大型頂尖的企業所採用，以協助企業主管充分發揮他們的英語潛能，而本書就是以 Leximodel 為基礎。

本章的目的在於介紹 Leximodel 的概念，以及運用方式。同時，也會針對如何藉由本書將這套學習法發揮最大效用加以說明。

閱讀完本章之後，各位應該能夠：

❏ 清楚了解 Leximodel 的概念，以及它對各位在學習上有什麼好處。
❏ 了解 chunks 、 set-phrases 和 word partnerships 的差別。
❏ 在任何文章中能自行找出 chunks 、 set-phrases 和 word partnerships 。
❏ 清楚了解學習 set-phrases 的困難點，以及如何克服這些困難。
❏ 清楚了解本書中的不同要素，以及如何將這些要素加以運用。

但在各位繼續下面的章節之前，我要先談談 Task 在本書的重要性。各位在前面的 Task 1 可以看到，我請各位先做個 Task ，即針對一些問題寫下自己的答案。希望各位都能按照我所說的，先做完 Task 再往下看。

每一單元都有許多經過嚴謹設計的 Task ，可以協助各位在不知不覺中吸收新的語言。此外，做 Task 時的思維過程要比答對與否來得重要，因此各位在練習時請務必按照既定的順序進行，且在做完練習之前先不要參照答案。

當然，為了節省時間，各位也可以略過 Task 、一鼓作氣地把整本書看完。不過，這麼做反而造成時間上的浪費，因為沒有做好必要的思維工作，本書就無法發揮最大的效果。請相信我的話，按部就班做 Task 準沒錯。

▶ The Leximodel

可預測度

　　在本節中，要向各位介紹 的是 Leximodel 學習法。 Leximodel 是一種看待語言的新方法，而且是以一個很簡單的概念為基礎：

> **Language consists of words which appear with other words.**
> 語言是由字串構成。

　　這種說法簡單易懂。 Leximodel 的基礎概念是從字串的層面來看語言，而非以文法和單字。為了讓各位明白這個概念，讓我們先來做 Task 2 吧！做完練習前先不要往下看。

Task 2

　　想一想，平常下列單字後面都會搭配什麼字？請寫在空格中。

listen _____

depend _____

English _____

financial _____

　　你很可能在第一個字後面填上 to ，在第二個字後面填上 on 。我猜得沒錯吧？因為只要用一套叫做 corpus linguistics 的軟體程式和運算技術，就可以在統計上發現 listen 後面接 to 的機率非常高（大約是 98.9%），而 depend 後面接 on 的機率也差不多。這表示 listen 和 depend 後面接的字幾乎是千篇一律，不會改變（listen 接

to ； depend 接 on）。由於機率非常高，所以我們可以把這兩個片語（listen to 、depend on）視爲固定（fixed）字串。由於它們是固定的，所以假如你所寫的不是 to 和 on，就可以說是寫錯了。

不過，接下來的兩個字（English 、 financial）後面會接什麼字就難預測得多，所以我猜不出來你在這兩個字的後面寫了什麼。但我可以在某個特定範圍內猜，你可能在 English 後面寫的是 class 、 book 、 teacher 、 email 或 grammar 等字；而在 financial 後面寫的是 department 、 news 、 planning 、 product 、 problems 或 stability 等。但我猜對的把握就比前面兩個字低了許多。爲什麼會這樣？因爲能正確預測 English 和 financial 後面接什麼字的準確率低了許多，很多字都有可能，而且每個字的機率相當。因此，我們可以說 English 和 financial 的字串是不固定的，而是流動的（fluid）。所以，與其把語言想成是由文法和字彙構成的，不妨把它想成是一個龐大的字串語料庫；裡面有些字串是固定的，有些字串則是流動的。

總而言之，根據可預測度，我們可以看出字串的固定性和流動性，如圖示：

The Spectrum of Predictability 可預測度

fixed 固定　←　listen to dependon　｜　English grammar financial news　→　fluid 流動

字串的可預測度是 Leximodel 的基礎，因此 Leximodel 的定義可以追加一句：

Language consists of words which appear with other words. These combinations of words can be placed along a spectrum of predictability, with fixed combinations at one end, and fluid combinations at the other.

語言由字串構成。每個字串根據可預測度來加以區分，可預測度愈高的一端是固定字串，可預測度愈低的一端是流動字串。

Chunks, set-phrases, 和 word partnerships

你可能在心裡兀自納悶：我曉得 Leximodel 是什麼了，可是這對學英文有何幫助？我如何知道哪些是固定字串，哪些是流動字串？就算知道了，對學英文來說會比較簡單嗎？別急，放輕鬆，從今天開始，英文就會愈學愈上手！

我們可以把所有的字串（稱之為 MWIs = multi-word items）分為三類：chunks、set-phrases 和 word partnerships。這些字沒有對等的中文譯名，所以請各位要記住這幾個英文字。現在，讓我們仔細看這三類字串，各位很快就會發現它們真的很容易了解與使用。

我們先來看第一類 MWIs：chunks。Chunks 字串有固定也有流動元素，listen to 就是個好例子：listen 的後面總是跟著 to（這是固定的），但有時候 listen 可以是 are listening、listened 或 have not been listening carefully enough（這些是流動的）。另一個好例子則是 give sth. to sb.。其中的 give 總是先接某物（sth.），然後再接 to，最後再接某人（sb.）。就這點來說，它是固定的。不過在這個 chunk 中，sth. 和 sb. 這兩個部分可以選擇的字很多，像是 give a raise to your staff（給員工加薪）和 give a presentation to your boss（向老闆做簡報）。看下列圖示你就懂了。

They [listened / are listening / have not been listening carefully enough] to the presentation.

We need to give [a proposal / a present / some thought] to [the client / Mandy / the new plan].

■ 部分為 fixed   ■ 部分為 fluid
（本書各類語庫會依顏色深淺區隔其流動性程度）

相信各位也能舉一反三，想出更多的例子。當然，我們還可以把 give sth. to sb. 寫成 give sb. sth.，但就變成了另一個 chunk。由此各位可看出 chunk 兼具固定和流動的元素。

而且 chunks 通常很短，是由 meaning words（意義字，如 listen、depend）加上 function words（功能字，如 to、on）所組成。相信你認識的 chunks 並不少，只是自己不知道罷了！所以，我們可以再來做另一個 Task，看看各位是不是已經懂得 chunks 的組成元素。請務必先作完 Task 3 再看答案，千萬不能作弊喔！

Task 3

請閱讀下列短文，找出所有的 chunks 並畫上底線。

Everyone is familiar with the experience of knowing what a word means, but not knowing how to use it accurately in a sentence. This is because words are nearly always used as part of an MWI. There are three kinds of MWI. The first is called a chunk. A chunk is a combination of words that is more or less fixed. Every time a word in the chunk is used, it must be used with its partner(s). Chunks combine fixed and fluid elements of language. When you learn a new word, you should learn the chunk. There are thousands of chunks in English. One way you can help yourself to improve your English is by noticing and keeping a database of the chunks you find as you read. You should also try to memorize as many as possible.

【中譯】　　每個人都有這樣的經驗：知道一個字的意思，卻不知道如何正確地用在句子中，這是因為每個字幾乎都必須當作 MWI 的一部分。MWI 可分為三類，第一類叫做 chunk。Chunk 幾乎是固定的字串，每當用到 chunk 的其中一字，該字的詞夥也得一併用上。Chunks 包含了語言中的固定元素和流動元素。在學習新字時，應該連帶學會它的 chunk。英文中有成千上萬的 chunks。閱讀時留意並記下所有的 chunks，將之彙整成語庫，最好還要盡量背起來，不失為加強英文的好法子。

Task **3** ▶參考答案

現在把你的答案與下面所列的語庫比較。假如你沒有找到那麼多 chunks，那就再看一次短文，看看是否能在文中找到語庫裡所有的 chunks。

電話和會議 **必備語庫 前言 1**

... be familiar with n.p. ...

... experience of Ving ...

... how to V ...

... be used as n.p. ...

... part of n.p. ...

... there are ...

... kinds of n.p. ...

... the first ...

... be called n.p. ...

... a combination of n.p. ...

... more or less ...

... every time + clause ...

... be used with n.p. ...

... combine sth. and sth. ...

... elements of n.p. ...

... thousands of n.p. ...

... in English ...

... help yourself to V ...

... keep a database of n.p. ...

... try to V ...

... as many as ...

... as many as possible ...

語庫小叮嚀

- 注意，語庫中的 chunks，be 動詞都以原形 be 表示，而非 is 或 are。
- 記下 chunks 時，前後都加上 ...（刪節號）。
- 注意有些 chunks 後面接 V（如：go、write 等原形動詞）或 Ving（如：going、writing 等），有的則接 n.p.（noun phrase，名詞片語）或 clause（子句）。這些將在「本書使用說明」中詳加解說。

好的，接下來我們要看的是第二類 MWIs：set-phrases。Set-phrases 比 chunks 固定，通常字串比較長，其中可能含有好幾個 chunks。而 set-phrases 通常有個開頭或結尾，或是兩者皆有，這表示有時候完整的句子也可以是 set-phrase。但 chunks 通常是由沒頭沒尾的片斷文字所組合。至於 set-phrases 則常見於電話和會議的用語。現在請參考下列語庫並做 Task 4。

Task 4

請看下列電話或一般會議中常見的 set-phrases，將你認得的勾選出來。

電話和會議 必備語庫 前言 2

Can you comment on this?

From my point of view,

In my opinion,

My own view is that + clause

My position is that + clause

My view is that + clause

One exception to this is n.p.

Take for example n.p.

There's no doubt in my mind that + clause

To give you an idea, look at n.p.

To give you an idea, take n.p.

To my way of thinking,

What's your position on this?

Where do you stand on this?

語庫小叮嚀

- 由於 set-phrases 是三類字串中固定性最高的，因此在學習時務必特別留意 set-phrases 的每個細節。稍後將詳加說明。
- 請注意，有些 set-phrases 以 n.p. 結尾，有的則以 clause 結尾。稍後也將詳加說明。

　　學會 set-phrases 的好處在於，使用時不必考慮文法：只需將這些 set-phrases 以固定字串的形式背起來，原原本本地照用即可。本書大部分的 Task 都和 set-phrases 有關，將於下一節對此詳加解說。現在，讓我們再繼續看第三類的 MWIs：word partnerships。

　　這三類 MWIs 中，以 word partnerships 的流動性最高，word partnerships 含有二個以上的意義字（不同於 chunks 的只含意義字和功能字），並且通常是「動詞＋形容詞＋名詞」或「名詞＋名詞」的組合。Word partnerships 會隨行業或談論的話題而有所改變，但各個產業所用的 chunks 和 set-phrases 都一樣。舉例來說，如果在製藥業工作，用到的 word partnerships 就會跟在資訊科技業服務的人士有所不同。現在，請接著做下面的 Task 5，就會瞭解我所說的意思。

Task 5

請依據範例，將會使用到下列各組 word partnerships 的產業寫下來。

❶
- government regulations
- patient response
- key opinion leader
- drug trial
- hospital budget
- patent law

產業名稱：　　　製藥業

❷
- risk assessment
- credit rating
- low inflation
- non-performing loan
- share price index
- bond portfolio

產業名稱：＿＿＿＿＿＿＿

❸
- bill of lading
- customs delay
- letter of credit
- shipment details
- shipping date
- customer service

產業名稱：＿＿＿＿＿＿＿

❹
- latest technology
- system problem
- input data
- user interface
- repetitive strain injury
- installation wizard

產業名稱：＿＿＿＿＿＿＿

Task 5 ▶ 參考答案

❷ 銀行和金融業
❸ 外銷／進出口業
❹ 資訊科技業

假如你在上述產業服務，你一定認得其中一些 word partnerships。

所以，現在我們對 Leximodel 的定義應該要再修正如下：

Language consists of words which appear with other words. These combinations can be categorized as chunks, set-phrases, and word partnerships, and placed along a spectrum of predictability, with fixed combinations at one end, and fluid combinations at the other.

語言由字串構成，所有的字串可以分成三大類—— chunks 、 set-phrases 和 word partnerships ，並且可依其可預測的程度區分，可預測度愈高的一端是固定字串，可預測度愈低的一端是流動字串。

所以，新的 Leximodel 可以圖示如下：

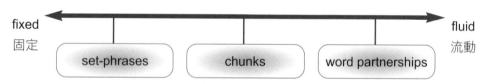

此外，只要致力學好 chunks ，文法就會有所精進，因為大部分的文法錯誤其實都源自於 chunks 寫錯；若專攻 set-phrases ，英語的使用功能就會增強，因為 set-phrases 都是功能性字串；若在 word partnerships 下功夫，字彙量就會擴增。因此，最後的 Leximodel 就可圖示如下：

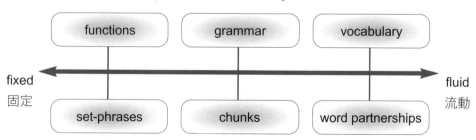

Leximodel 的優點及其對於學習英文的妙用，就在於說、寫英文時，均無須再為文法規則傷透腦筋。學習英文時，首要之務是建立 chunks、set-phrases 和 word partnerships 的語料庫，多學多益。而不是死背文法規則，還得苦思如何將單字套用到文法中。這三類 MWIs 用來輕而易舉，而且更符合人腦記憶和使用語言的習慣。現在，我們再來做最後一個 Task，以確認完全了解 Leximodel 的概念，並驗證這項學習法的簡單好用。切記在完成 Task 之前，先不要看語庫。

Task 6

請看以下電話會議中的簡短對話和翻譯，然後以三種不同顏色的筆分別將所有的 chunks、set-phrases 和 word partnerships 畫上底線。最後，請依各類字串的範例完成後頁的分類表。

Jackie: So my suggestion here is that we hold off with the new project until we get more specific details from the client. Mike, what do you think?

Mike: As I see it, we don't have any real alternative. We can't go ahead because the specs we've got don't match. We need clarification before we can proceed.

Jackie: I think you're right. Julian, what's your view?

Julian: Well, I'm not sure. I know there's a slight problem with the specs, but in my opinion there are still other things we can work on until we get greater clarification.

Jackie: What do you mean by that?

Julian: Well, put simply, we can still prepare product samples for the client, show them the color, the materials. In any case, we don't want to delay the project if we can help it, because a delay is going to cost us, not the client.

Tracy: I agree completely. I would prefer to continue with the project. I don't think we should hold off the whole thing just because the specs are not clear. To put it bluntly, we can clear them up in thirty minutes with a quick phone call.

Mike: So you want us to carry on and ignore the problems with the specs? To be quite frank, I think we're making a serious mistake if we think the specs are not important.

Tracy: I'm afraid there seems to have been a slight misunderstanding. Of course I think the specs are important, but they don't need to hold everything else up. I can call the chief engineer at the client side this afternoon and get clarification on the specs.

Mike: Well, I think we should wait until we clear up the problems with the specs.

Julian: I'm afraid I have to disagree, Mike. Couldn't we still get on with the marketing plan for the project? The specs aren't going to change that much, and any marketing plan we come up with is not going to change that much if the specs change, right?

【中譯】

賈　姬：那麼我這邊的建議就是先暫停這個新案子，等從客戶那裡拿到更明確的細節再說。麥克，你覺得怎麼樣？

麥　克：我是覺得我們沒別的選擇了。我們不能直接做，因為手上的規格不吻合。我們需要先搞清楚，才能開始著手。

賈　姬：我覺得你說得沒錯。朱里安，你的看法呢？

朱里安：呃，我不確定。我知道規格是有一點問題，但在我看來，在對方說清楚之前，我們還是有其他事可以進行。

賈　姬：怎麼說？

朱里安：這麼說吧，我們還是可以幫客戶準備產品樣本，給他們看顏色、材料。無論如何，有辦法的話這個案子最好不要拖，因為拖延所導致的成本是由我們負擔，而不是客戶。

崔　西：我完全同意。我比較贊成繼續做這個案子。我覺得不應該因為規格不明而將整個案子停擺。恕我直言，規格的事只需一通電話，30 分鐘就可以很快釐清了。

麥　克：所以你們希望大家繼續做下去，不管規格問題嗎？坦白講，我覺得要是小看規格問題，可就大錯特錯了。

崔　西：　你恐怕是有一點誤會了。我當然也覺得規格很重要，但是沒必要把其他事情全部停擺。我可以今天下午就打電話給客戶那邊的總工程師，把規格問清楚。

麥　克：　我是覺得我們應該等規格問題解決了再說。

朱里安：　麥克，我恐怕無法贊成。難道我們就不能繼續做案子的行銷計畫嗎？就算規格要改也不會改多少，而且無論我們想出什麼行銷計畫，都不會因為規格改了而受影響，對吧？

set-phrases	chunks	word partnerships
So my suggestion here is that ...	*... hold off with ...*	*new project*

Task 6 ▶參考答案

請利用下面的必備語庫來核對答案。

電話和會議 必備語庫 前言 3

set-phrases	chunks	word partnerships
So my suggestion here is that ...	... hold off with ...	new project
What do you think?	... get sth. from ...	specific details
As I see it, ...	... go ahead ...	real alternative
I think you're right.	... problem with ...	slight problem
What's your view?	... work on ...	greater clarification
Well, I'm not sure.	... prepare sth. for sb. ...	prepare product samples
... in my opinion, ...	... the client ...	quick phone call
What do you mean by that?	... want to ...	serious mistake
Well, put simply, ...	... continue with ...	chief engineer
I agree completely.	... hold off ...	marketing plan
I would prefer to ...	... the whole thing ...	
To put it bluntly, ...	... clear sth. up ...	
So you want us to ...	... in thirty minutes ...	
To be quite frank, ...	... carry on ...	
I'm afraid there seems to have been a slight misunderstanding.	... need to ...	
I'm afraid I have to disagree.	... hold everything up ...	
	... at the client side ...	
	... this afternoon ...	
	... the specs ...	
	... get on with ...	
	... come up with ...	

語庫小叮嚀

- 注意，set-phrases 通常以大寫開頭，或以句號結尾。而刪節號（...）則代表句子的流動部分。
- 注意，chunks 的開頭和結尾都有刪節號，表示 chunks 為句子的中間部分。
- 注意，word partnerships 均由兩個以上的意義字所組成。

　　假如你的答案沒有這麼完整，不必擔心。只要多加練習，就能找出文中所有的固定元素。不過有一件事是可以確定的：等到你能找出這麼多 MWIs 時，就表示你的英文已經到達登峰造極的境界了！相信很快你便能擁有這樣的英文能力。於本書末尾，我會請各位再做一次這個 Task，來驗證自己的學習成果。如果有時間的話，各位不妨找一篇英文文章，像是以英文為母語的人所寫的電子郵件，或是雜誌和網路上的文章，然後用它來做同樣的練習，想必會熟能生巧哦！

▶ 本書使用說明

　　到目前為止，我猜各位大概會覺得 Leximodel 似乎是個不錯的概念，但腹中仍有疑問，對吧？對於各位可能會有的問題，我來看看能否提供解答。

● 我該如何實際運用 Leximodel 學英文？為什麼 Leximodel 和我以前碰到的英文教法截然不同？

　　簡而言之，我的答案是：只要知道字詞的組合和這些組合的固定程度，就能簡化英語學習的過程，同時大幅減少犯錯的機率。

　　以前的教學法教你學好文法，然後套用句子，邊寫邊造句。用這方法寫作不僅有如牛步，而且稍不小心便錯誤百出，想必各位早就有切身體驗了。現在只要用 Leximodel 建立 chunks、set-phrases 和 word partnerships 語庫，接著只需背起來就能學會英文寫作了。

● 這本書如何以 Leximodel 教學？

　　本書除了介紹如何學習和運用電話會議和一般會議中最常出現的固定字串（chunks、set-phrases 和 word partnerships，但絕大多數是 set-phrases）之外，並教各位如何留意和記下每天所看到的英文，來增強英文基礎。

● 為什麼要留意字串中所有的字，很重要嗎？

　　不知何故，大多數人對眼前的英文視而不見，分明擺在面前卻仍然視若無睹，時常緊盯著字詞的意思，卻忽略了傳達字義的方法。雖然每天所瀏覽的固定 MWI 多不勝數，但其實這些 MWI 只不過是組成固定而又反覆出現的字串罷了。很多其他種類的語言都有這種現象。不如這樣吧，我們來做個實驗，各位就會知道我說的是真是假。現在請做下面的 Task 7。

Task 7

請看下列的 set-phrases，並選出正確的。

❑ Regarding the report you sent me ...
❑ Regarding to the report you sent me ...
❑ Regards to the report you sent me ...
❑ With regards the report you sent ...
❑ To regard the report you sent me ...
❑ Regard to the report you sent me ...

姑且不論所選的答案為何，我敢說各位一定覺得這題很難作答。我們可能每天都會看到這個 set-phrase，卻從來沒有仔細留意它當中的每一個字（其實第一個 set-phrase 是正確答案，其餘都是錯的！）。說到這兒，我要給各位學習 set-phrase 時的第一個忠告：

雖然各位應該對所接觸到的英文加強注意，但仿效的文字必須出自以英文為母語的人士之手。所謂的「以英文為母語的人士」，指的是美國人、英國人、澳洲人、紐西蘭人、加拿大人或南非人。如果英文非其母語，就算是老闆或十年前在美國念過博士、英文能力公認好得沒話說的公司同事，也信不過。

務必只仿效以英文為母語人士的用語示範。

如果多留意每天接觸到的固定字串，久而久之一定會記起來，轉化成自己英文基礎的一部分，這可是諸多文獻可考的事實。只需多加留意閱讀時所遇到的 MWI，亦可提升學習效率。Leximodel 正能幫助各位達到這項目標。

● 需要小心哪些問題？

本書中許多 Task 的目的，即在於幫助各位克服學 set-phrases 時所遇到的問題。學 set-phrases 的要領在於：務必留意 set-phrases 中所有的字。

　　從 Task 7 中，各位或許已發現自己其實不如想像中那麼仔細留意 set-phrases 中所有的字。接下來我要更確切地告訴各位學 set-phrases 時的注意事項，這些注意事項對於學習 set-phrases 而言非常重要，請勿草率閱讀。學習和使用 set-phrases 時，需要注意的細節有四大類：

❶ 短字（如 a、the、to、in、at、on 和 but）。這些字很難記，但瞭解這點之後，便可說是跨出了一大步。 Set-phrases 極為固定，用錯一個短字，整個 set-phrase 都會改變，等於是寫錯了。

❷ 字尾（有些字的字尾是 -ed，有些是 -ing，有些是 -ment，有些字尾為 -s，有些字尾則不加 -s）。字尾改變了，字的意思也會隨之改變。 Set-phrase 極為固定，寫錯其中一字的字尾，整個 set-phrase 都會改變，也等於是寫錯了。

❸ Set-phrases 的結尾（有的 set-phrase 以 clause 結尾，有的以 n. p. 結尾，有的以 V 結尾，有的則以 Ving 結尾），我們稱之為 code。許多人犯錯，問題即出在句子中 set-phrases 與其他部分的銜接之處。學習 set-phrases 時，必須將 code 當作 set-phrases 的一部分一併背起來。 Set-phrases 極為固定， code 寫錯，整個 set-phrase 都會改變，亦等於是寫錯了

❹ 完整的 set-phrases。 Set-phrase 是固定的單位，所以必須完整地加以使用，不能只用前半部或其中幾個字而已。

　　說明至此，請各位再做下面的 Task 8，以確認能夠掌握 code 的用法。

Task　8

　　請看以下對 code 的定義，然後將下列字串分門別類填入表格中。其中已將第一個字串所屬的類別示範如下。

■ clause ＝ （子句），你在學校大概已經學過， clause 一定包含主詞和動詞。
　　　　　例如：I need your help.、 She is on leave.、 We are closing the department.、 What is your estimate? 等。

■ n. p.　= noun phrase（名詞片語），這其實就是 word partnership，但是不含動詞或主詞。例如：financial news、cost reduction、media review data、joint stock company 等。

■ V　　= verb（動詞）。和 clause 的不同之處在於，V 不包含主詞。

■ Ving　= verb ending in -ing（以 -ing 結尾的動詞）。以前各位的老師可能稱之為動名詞，但 Ving 只是看起來像名詞的動詞。

- ~~bill of lading~~
- customer complaint
- decide
- did you remember
- do
- doing
- go
- great presentation
- having
- he is not
- help
- helping
- I'm having a meeting
- John wants to see you
- knowing
- look after
- our market share
- see
- sending
- talking
- we need some more data
- wrong figures
- you may remember
- your new client

clause	n.p.	V	Ving
	● *bill of lading*		

Task 8 ▶參考答案

請利用下面的必備語庫來核對答案。

電話和會議 **必備語庫 前言 4**

clause	n.p.	V	Ving
● did you remember	● bill of lading	● decide	● doing
● he is not	● customer complaint	● do	● having
● I'm having a meeting	● great presentation	● go	● helping
● John wants to see you	● our market share	● help	● knowing
● we need some more data	● wrong figures	● look after	● sending
● you may remember	● your new client	● see	● talking

語庫小叮嚀

- 注意 clause（子句）的 verb（動詞）前面一定要有主詞。
- 注意 noun phrases（名詞片語）基本上即為 word partnerships。

總而言之，學習 set-phrases 時，容易出錯的主要問題有：

1. 短字
2. 字尾
3. Set-phrases 的結尾
4. 完整的 set-phrase

並不會太困難，對吧？

如果沒有文法規則可循，我怎麼知道自己的 set-phrases 用法正確無誤？

關於這點，讀或寫在這方面要比說來得容易。說話時要仰賴記憶，所以會有點困難。不過，本書採用了兩種工具來幫各位簡化這個過程。

1. 學習目標記錄表。本書的附錄有一份「學習目標記錄表」。各位在開始拿本書來練習前，應該先多印幾份學習目標記錄表。由於要學的 set-phrases 和 word partnerships 有很多，可以選擇幾個來作重點學習。從各單元的語庫中，將想要學習的用語列在記錄表上。建議每週挑出 10 個用語加以學習。

2. MP3 音檔。在開會時，發音清楚是留給對方好印象的關鍵之一，所以本書也會把練習重點專注在發音方面。各位會一直需要用到 MP3 音檔，這不僅對發音有所幫助，也有益於加強聽力，並且會讓學習更有趣、更有效。下載 MP3 音檔後，可以用 MP3 播放機隨聽隨學；也可以用 MP3 播放機錄下自己的發音，然後和本書提供的錄音進行比較。請盡量模仿 MP3 音檔的發音，並確定自己所唸的 set-phrases 與之完全吻合。利用 MP3 音檔練習各位所挑出和列在記錄表上的 set-phrases，每天花 10 分鐘聆聽和複誦，會比禮拜天晚上花 2 個小時練習還來得有效。

因此，學習 set-phrases 的時候，只要專心學習書中的必備語庫和 MP3 中的音檔就好，不必擔心文法規則。雖然看我說得簡單，事實上也確實如此，畢竟熟能生巧準沒錯。現在請再做下面的 Task 9，記住，做完之後再往下看答案。

Task 9 **02**

請聽 MP3 中的句子，然後將你實際聽到的內容寫在下面。

1. _____

2. _____

3. _____

4. _____

5. _____

6. _____

7. _____

Task **9** ▶參考答案

請核對實際聽到的內容是否如下。

1. It seem to me that the market is growing.
2. There's not doubt in my mind that we should increase our price.
3. To my opinion, the red one is better.
4. For my way of thinking, the blue one is not so good.
5. Where do you stand?
6. Can you tell me your views on the situation is bad?
7. Do you have any idea about this?

各位可能會覺得這些句子有些怪，別急，請繼續做 Task 10。

Task **10**

　　請將「電話和會議必備語庫前言 3」中的 set-phrases 和上題實際聽到的答案作比較。各位能看出兩者有什麼不同嗎？請看以下範例，在實際聽到的句子下面寫出正確的句子，並在正確句子的後面標示錯誤原因的編號（錯誤的原因有： 1. 短字； 2. 字尾； 3. Set-phrases 的結尾； 4. 完整的 set-phrase）。

1. It seem to me that the market is growing.

It seems to me that the market is growing.　　　　　　(2)

2. There's not doubt in my mind that we should increase our price.

_____

3. To my opinion, the red one is better.

_____

4. For my way of thinking, the blue one is not so good.

_____

5. Where do you stand?

_____

6. Can you tell me your views on the situation is bad?

_____

7. Do you have any idea about this?

_____

Task 10 ▶ 參考答案

請核對寫出的正確句子和錯誤原因的編號是否如下。

2. *There's no doubt in my mind that we should increase our price.* （2）
3. *In my opinion, the red one is better.* （1）
4. *To my way of thinking, the blue one is not so good.* （1）
5. *Where do you stand on this?* （4）
6. *Can you tell me your views on the bad situation?* （3）
7. *Do you have any ideas about this?* （2）

　　如果寫出的答案和參考答案南轅北轍的話，請重新複習本節，並且特別注意 Task 8 和關於 set-phrases 四個細節問題的解說。另外也可再閱讀一遍 Task 6 電話會議的範例，參考其中 set-phrases 的用法。如有必要，請現在就回頭複習。本書中許多 Task 會幫各位將注意力集中在 set-phrases 的類似細節上，各位只須詳讀、多聽、作答和核對答案，無須擔心背後原因。

● 本書的架構為何？

本書分為六個單元，每個單元將焦點集中於一種類型的會議策略和用語。首先 Unit 1 是電話會議和一般會議的概要介紹，包括節省時間和精力的秘訣；然後 Unit 2 是專談展開電話會議的程序。接下來的三個單元分別著重在三種不同的電話會議或一般會議，依序是：Unit 3 的資訊型會議、Unit 4 的解決問題型會議，還有 Unit 5 的規畫和決策型會議，每個單元的教學重點在於每一型會議的必備用語。至於，最後的 Unit 6 重點則為主持電話會議或一般會議的用語和技巧。

每個單元大約分成兩部分：每一部分都會提供該單元主題所需的技巧和用語，此外，在每個單元的最後則為會議的各項基本技巧，針對一般用語和字彙的擴增提供系統化的練習。現在就請先花點時間閱覽本書的目錄，以熟悉未來的學習方向。

本書介紹的字串大都是以 set-phrases 的形式呈現，因為 set-phrases 是字串中執行功能的部分，也就是讓我們達成溝通目的的部分。更何況，無論是電話會議或一般商務會議，目的都是為了要把事情辦成。至於這些 set-phrases，則會彙整在每個單元的「電話和開會必備語庫」，各位可以拿 MP3 音檔當作練習的範本。勤加利用 MP3 所提供的聽力素材，對學習效果的增益極大。本書最後的附錄一將提供各單元的「電話和開會必備語庫」一覽表，方便各位使用。

此外，MP3 音檔中附有電話會議和一般會議的範例，供各位鍛鍊聽力和溝通技巧。除非必要，聆聽時請不要對照書上所列的對話台詞，而是仔細聆聽音檔中講者的用語和語調，注意講者和對方的互動。

● 我該如何利用本書達到最佳學習效果？

為了達到最佳學習效果，謹提供以下幾個學習訣竅：

1. 請按照單元的編排閱讀本書。為了提供更多記憶 set-phrases 的機會，本書會反覆提到一些語言和概念，因此倘若一開始有不解之處，請耐心看下去，多半念到本書後面的章節時自然就會恍然大悟。

2. 如果各位正好在閱讀本書的期間有機會參加電話會議或一般會議，試著聆聽已經讀過的語句，並同時運用一些已經學過的 set-phrases。

3. 每個 Task 都不放過。這些 Task 有助於記憶本書的字串，亦可加強各位對這些字串的理解，所以不可輕忽。

4. 建議各位在做 Task 時以鉛筆做答。如此，即使寫錯也還可擦掉再試一次。

5. 做分類 Task 時（請見 Unit 2 的 Task 2.2），只需在每個 set-phrase 旁加註記號或標示英文字母即可。但建議各位有空時，還是將 set-phrases 抄在正確的一欄中。各位還記得當初是怎麼學中文的嗎？沒錯！抄寫能夠加深印象。

6. 請利用本書附錄的「學習目標記錄表」追蹤自己的學習狀況，如此有助於挑出想在會議中使用的字串。關於如何挑選字串，提供各位以下幾點建議：

　❑ 選擇難度高、陌生或新的字串。
　❑ 如果可以的話，避免使用你已經知道或覺得運用自如的字串。
　❑ 特意使用這些新的字串。

7. 如果各位想提升英文能力的決心夠堅定，建議和同事組成 K 書會，一同閱讀本書和做 Task。

● 在開始研讀本書之前，還有哪些須知？

Yes, you can do it!

　開始閱讀 Unit 1 前，請先回到前言的「學習目標」，回顧一下 Task 1 的學習目標，勾出各位認為已經達成的項目。希望所有目標都能夠達成並且打勾，如果沒有，請重新閱讀相關段落。

　祝學習有成，開會愉快！

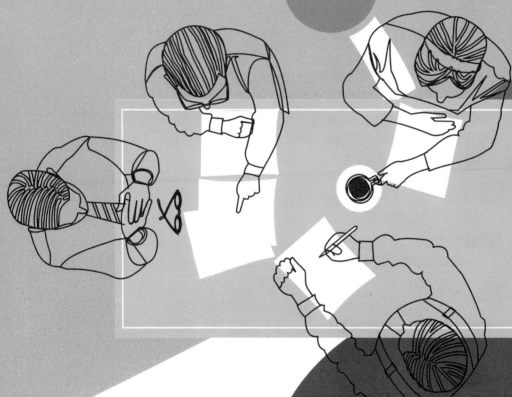

Unit 1

有效會議的
重要事項

*Effective Conference
Calls and Meetings*

引言與學習目標

　　大部分有經驗的商務人士都知道，工作時所出席的會議，泰半是在浪費時間。大家在開會時，一定都有過這樣的經驗：會開到一半的時候，暗自希望把時間花在其他較有生產力的事上，而非開會。因為開會是效率很低的做事方法，在開會時根本無法分身去做其他比較重要的事，而且不只你一個人如此，其他開會的每一個人皆是如此。從經濟面來考量，如果把開會的所有人力時數加總起來，除以大家原本可以用來完成別項事務的人力時數，然後將所得出的數字，與開會得出的結果或會議中完成的事項相比，你就會發現開會的投資報酬率其實微乎其微。換做是財務專家，也絕不會建議你把金錢投資在開會上！

　　話雖如此，電話會議和一般會議仍有其必要之處。因開會而將大家聚集在一起，在大家的互動中激盪、發展出新的商業點子，同時更促成了人與人之間的信任關係，這層關係則是所有商業活動、團隊合作的基礎。

　　因此，在本單元將介紹給各位一些提高電話會議和一般會議效率的秘訣，幫助各位提升工作時效的投資報酬率。

　　在本單元的學習結束時，各位應該達成的學習目標如下：

❏ 了解有效召開電話會議和一般會議的最佳作法等訣竅 。
❏ 學會一些基本的電話用語 。
❏ 學會一些可用來打電話留言和記下對方留言的 set-phrases 。
❏ 練習過數字和字母的聽力和發音。

八項有效開會的最佳訣竅

先就各位所參加之電話會議和一般會議的經驗來做練習。請回想各位在工作上至今開過最成功的電話會議和一般會議，這些會議之所以成功，有哪些共通點呢？

Task 1.1

成功的電話會議有哪些特點？請參照範例所勾選出的其中一項特點，在下列選項的方格中勾選出適合的特點。若想到其他特點，也可以寫在下面的空欄中。

have	a clear agenda	✓
	a problem	
	a break	
	a clear purpose	
	a nice cup of tea	
	a leader for each team	
	a vacation	
	clear action points	
	cutting edge technology	
	something to say	
	clear start and finish times	
	a "no interruptions" policy	

Task 1.1 ▶參考答案

以下是一些最能提高電話會議和一般會議效率的建議作法。不過，這些建議的排序先後與其重要性並無關連。

● 目的設定清楚

　　假如你有決定是否安排電話會議的權限，首先要做的便是思考有無開會的必要。倘若開會的目的僅是為了分享資訊，那麼這場會議便絕對是浪費時間了。若要分享資訊，透過電子郵件、報告、表格等同樣可以達成目的。但如果你沒有開會與否的決定權卻又必須參加會議，那麼請思考你是否真有必要參加這場會議。你對會中討論的主題是否會有貢獻？還是其實另外派人去開會，然後請他事後向你報告會比較好？

　　在開會之前，不僅會議目的必須設定清楚，也必須確定與會的每一位都知道開會的目的為何，這就是清楚安排議程的重要所在。

● 議程清楚

　　議程要盡量維持精簡，只安排兩、三項議題即可。確定所有與會的人都預先拿到一份議程表，並準備好對各項討論議題所欲提獻的想法。議程表上面應該表明會議目的，讓每一位與會者都能朝著相同的目標邁進，並列出所有預計參加會議者的名單，如此大家便能知道你主持的這一場會議中會有哪些人在場。記住，除非要召開的是大家不會見到面的語音會議，否則在開會前便應該讓大家知道有哪些人會出席。開會之前拿到議程還有一個好處，那就是如果事先知道要討論的議題，就可以預先準備會用到的語句。你可以先查好開會時可能用到或聽到的詞彙。本書後面便有一些 set-phrases 供你參考。

　　開會時請按照議程進行，盡量不要脫離主題。議程上沒有的項目就不要討論，同時也敦促其他人不要離題。

● 行動計畫清楚

　　按照議程召開會議時，每一項議題均應討論出明確的行動計畫，然後才接續下一個議題的討論。所謂明確的行動計畫，即包括預定好三個 wh-：who、what、when，也就是何人該做何事、應於何時完成，即指定人員負責計畫的執行，並預定完成日期。關於這方面的訣竅，以及可用來清楚設定行動計畫的用語，將於 Unit 6 詳加介紹。

● 開始和結束時間明確

由於參加會議的人員或許分散在世界各地，而且工作時區不同，所以會議務必準時開始、準時結束。開會時間對你來說可能很方便，但對其他與會者來說卻可能是在午夜或甚至更晚，如果大家準時開會，那些人會很感謝。要是開會遲到，而讓其他人等你，這就形同浪費時間了。所以，千萬不要浪費其他人的時間！確定會議準時結束，並且在會議結束前討論完議程中的所有議題。

● 言之有物

開一般會議時是可以不發表意見的，你可以聽人家的討論然後做筆記，安安靜靜地參與會議。但在電話會議中你得要有所貢獻，好讓大家知道你的存在！由於文化上的差異，有些中文人士對於用英文就討論事項、提出看法或挑戰他人意見時，常感到不自在，但請記住的是，西方人會期望每一位與會者能公平參與會議。有想法就表達出來，有建議就提出來；不同意對方的話就直說，不懂對方的意思就請對方解釋。如果覺得有人誤解你的意思，就要指正對方；如果覺得有人對某件事的理解有誤，就要打斷討論更正他。

本書的後續單元將介紹各位不失禮貌又恰到好處的用語，來達到這些目的。

● 規定開會時「請勿干擾」

現代通訊科技讓我們彼此之間的聯繫變得更容易，卻也可能導致我們彼此之間的干擾，這點缺憾只能讓人搖頭興嘆。我們有手機，不表示我們一天二十四小時都得隨時待命，等著別人打電話來談公事。我們有筆記型電腦和無線網路連結，不表示我們就得不斷查詢電子郵件信箱、一有來信就得馬上回覆。可惜許多商務人士似乎都忘了這一點，尤其在召開電話會議和一般會議時更是如此。我們應該把科技當工具才對，而不是變成科技的奴隸。

開會時請記得關掉手機、切斷筆記型電腦的網路連線並且關掉 PDA。你現在正在開會，不該心有旁鶩。請把心思放在會議的討論主題，尊重會議的其他在場人士，別讓他們等你處理一通電話或一封電子郵件。你可能在講電話時錯過了一些議題的重要資訊，若為你而複述一遍，這對他人而言並不公平。而且，如果是重要電話，別擔心，對方會再打一次的。養成請對方在語音信箱留言的習慣，然後等你有空時便可聯絡他們。別讓客戶霸佔了你的時間。

永遠記住，在商場上沒有緊急大事。我們不是要拯救生命或搶救地球，有些事情多等幾個小時沒關係。

● 使用最先進的科技

我在本書中不會推薦任何一家廠牌的語音或視訊會議設備，因為有些製造廠商是我的客戶，我可不想惹毛任何一家廠商！

不過要提醒各位使用高科技設備時容易忘記的一件事，那就是除非自己親手關掉開關，否則千萬不要以為機器已經關了。

我在教電話會議的課堂上，每次都會播放一個以前朋友寄給我的網路影片給學生看。影片中有四組人要進行視訊會議，當時大家正在等著會議開始。就在大家等候其中一方連線進入視訊會議時，一名年輕貌美、留著一頭金色秀髮的女子卻露出坐立難安的樣子。她的老闆是一名上了年紀的先生，人在另一個地方，另外還有一些同事也位於不同的地方，但大家都注意到了女子的舉動並開始觀察她。女子不知道自己的視訊連結已經連上：因為她自己看不到別人，便也以為別人也看不到她。後來她越來越煩躁，突然決定解下胸罩，原來是胸罩在刮身體。就在她解下胸罩的時候，她的「本錢」全部曝光在其他小組成員的眼前。她的老闆大吃一驚，同事們也都尷尬的大笑。她總算連接上對方的視訊畫面時，她向大家道歉，說自己這端的連線出了點技術性問題。她老闆說：「妳是指妳的胸罩嗎？」年輕女子頓時難堪地想找個地洞鑽下去。

雖然這段影片引人發笑，但可想而知那名年輕女子的自尊和形象受到多大的損害。所以千萬別忘了，除非肯定已經切斷連線，否則便要假設每一台視訊機器都是處於連線狀態。有這些高科技設備在場時，絕對不要說出或做出平常私底下才會說或做的事。

● 指定組長

　　如同一般會議需要主持人一樣，電話會議的各個小組最好也都指派一名組長。因為各個小組若沒有組長，會議就不知道該由誰主導，也不清楚各項議題該由誰負責。會議中的組長所扮演的某些重要角色，和會議主持人所扮演的角色大同小異。現在請各位做下面的 Task，就會了解組長所擔負的責任。

Task 1.2

請利用方框中的參考語彙，選取適當者填入空格以完成以下這篇概要。

The Leader's Role

The leader's job is to manage _____*the call*_____, including the

_____(1)_____ and the _____(2)_____ involved. The leader has to

get the call _____(3)_____, make sure the _____(4)_____ of the call is

clear, make sure that everyone in his or her team sticks to the _____(5)_____,

and establish clear _____(6)_____ and _____(7)_____.

started	technology	people	purpose
the call	due dates	action points	agenda

Task 1.2 ▶ 參考答案

The Leader's Role

The leader's job is to manage the call, including the <u>technology</u> and the <u>people</u> involved. The leader has to get the call <u>started</u>, make sure the <u>purpose</u> of the call is clear, make sure that everyone in his or her team sticks to the <u>agenda</u>, and establish clear <u>action points</u> and <u>due dates</u>.

組長的角色

組長的工作是管理有關會議的一切事項,其中也包括技術層面和相關人員。組長必須引導電話會議的開展,確定召開會議的目的,確認小組成員皆能按照議程進行討論,並且清楚設定行動事項和完成日期。

在 Unit 1 和 Unit 6 中將介紹如何帶領小組進行電話會議,以及主持會議時所需的語彙和技巧。

最後,在繼續往下閱讀之前,要特別提醒各位,召開電話會議和一般會議不時會遇到問題,那是因為會議是一種群體活動。意思就是,除非電話會議和一般會議中的所有人都知道我所提到的訣竅,否則單靠你一個人的力量實踐我所說的最佳作法,而其他與會者卻不然時,那也只會徒勞無功。因為主持會議的經理不見得知道所謂的最佳作法。不過,各位可以在公司廣為宣傳這些訣竅,如果自己本身就是經理,還可以要求員工運用這些訣竅。倘若你才剛進入職場,也可以在拓展生涯的同時將這些訣竅付諸實踐。

電話應答

　　所有的電話會議都是從一通簡單的電話開始進行，因此在本節中我們將來學習一些基本的電話語言，用以接電話、留言等。我們就從一個聽力練習開始吧。記住，現在先不要看電話的對照文。

Task 1.3 聽力 1.1 和 1.2

請聽兩通電話，並回答下列問題：
- 第一通電話：電話是誰打的？她想找誰？
- 第二通電話：電話是誰打的？他想找誰？

Task 1.3 ▶ 參考答案

　　在第一通電話中，打電話來的是快樂旅行社的瑪莉，她要找貝爾公司的麥克，但麥克正在開會，所以她留了話，請麥克回電。

　　在第二通電話中，是麥克回電給瑪莉。接電話的人告訴麥克，瑪莉在另一個房間，然後將麥克的電話轉接給瑪莉了。

　　現在我們來看一下打這類電話時可以使用的語彙。和某人在電話上取得聯繫時有四組 set-phrases 可用，分別是：打電話（making the call），接電話（taking the call），留言（leaving a message）和記錄留言（taking a message）的 set-phrases。

Task 1.2

　　將下面的 set-phrases 分類，在各個 set-phrase 旁邊寫上所屬的類別字母（如 M、C、L 和 T）。請參考範例所示。

M = Making the call	C = Taking the call	L = Leaving a message	T = Taking a message

T	Anything else?
	Can I have your name, please?
	Can I leave a message?
	Can I take a message?
	Can I speak to X?
	Could I speak to X please?
	Could you give her a message?
	Could you read that back to me?
	Could you repeat that, please?
	Could you take a message?
	Have you got that?
	Hello, my name's X and I'm calling from Y.
	Hold on please.
	I'd like to speak to X please.
	I'll call back later.
	I'll hold.
	I'll just put you through.
	I'm afraid he's off sick.
	I'm afraid he's on the other line.
	I'm afraid he's tied up at the moment.
	I'm afraid he's unavailable at the moment.
	I'm afraid she's in a meeting.
	I'm afraid she's not here just now.
	Is X there please?
	Let me read that back to you.
	OK, go ahead please.
	Ready?
	Speaking.
	This is X speaking.
	Would you like to leave a message?
	X here.
	Can I help you?
	Let me put you through.
	This is X from Y.

Task 1.4 ▶參考答案

請利用下面的必備語庫檢查答案，然後閱讀語庫解析。

電話和會議 *必備語庫* 1.1

Making the call

Is X there please?

Can I speak to X?

Could I speak to X please?

I'd like to speak to X please.

X here.

This is X speaking.

This is X from Y.

Hello, my name's X and I'm calling from Y.

I'll call back later.

I'll hold.

Taking the call

Can I help you?

Hold on please.

I'll just put you through.

Let me put you through.

I'm afraid he's off sick.

I'm afraid he's on the other line.

I'm afraid he's tied up at the moment.

I'm afraid he's unavailable at the moment.

I'm afraid she's in a meeting.

I'm afraid she's not here just now.

Speaking.

This is X speaking.

X here.

Leaving a message

Can I leave a message?

Could you take a message?

Could you give her a message?

Ready?

Could you read that back to me?

Have you got that?

Taking a message

Can I take a message?

Would you like to leave a message?

Can I have your name, please?

OK, go ahead please.

Could you repeat that, please?

Let me read that back to you.

Anything else?

語庫解析

● Making the call 打電話

Is X there please?	
Can I speak to X?	這些 set-phrases 是按照禮貌程度排列，越
Could I speak to X please?	前面的說法越不正式，越後面的則越有禮
I'd like to speak to X please.	貌。打電話找人時請用這些 set-phrases。

X here.	
This is X speaking.	這些 set-phrases 是按照禮貌程度排列，越
This is X from Y.	前面的說法越不正式，越後面的則越有禮
Hello, my name's X and I'm calling from Y.	貌。表明來歷及公司名稱時請用這些 set-phrases。

● Taking the call 接電話

Can I help you?

這個 set-phrase 用於接聽電話時，比簡短的 Yes?或 Hello?有禮貌。

Hold on please.

永遠記得說 Hold on please，而不要說 Wait a minute。雖然 Wait a minute 在中文顯得較有禮貌，但翻成英文就過於直接，所以請不要這麼用。

I'll just put you through.
Let me put you through.

這兩個 set-phrases 可用於將電話轉給某人。

I'm afraid he's off sick.
I'm afraid he's on the other line.
I'm afraid he's tied up at the moment.
I'm afraid he's unavailable at the moment.
I'm afraid she's in a meeting.
I'm afraid she's not here just now.

這些 set-phrases 可用於向人解釋某人無法接聽電話。

Speaking.
This is X speaking.
X here.

這些 set-phrases 可用於表明自己是何許人。不要說 I am X，這句英文在電話上聽起來很怪。

● Leaving a message 留言

Can I leave a message?

Could you take a message?

Could you give her a message?

這些 set-phrases 是按照禮貌程度排列，越前面的說法越不正式，越後面的則越有禮貌。

Ready?

Could you read that back to me?

Have you got that?

留言之前可以先問 Ready? 看對方手邊有沒有筆，這樣比較有禮貌。留完言之後，可以說 Have you got that? 看對方是否正確記下了你的話。

● Taking a message 記錄留言

OK, go ahead please.

準備好幫對方記錄留言時可以用這個 set-phrase。

Could you repeat that, please?

沒聽懂對方的話時可用這個 set-phrase。

Anything else?

記錄好留言時可以用這個 set-phrase。

Task 1.5 聽力 1.3 05

請利用聽力 1.3，練習必備語庫 1.1 中 set-phrases 的發音。

Task 1.5 ▶ 參考答案

　　如希望講電話時語氣親切、專業又流利，必須注意兩個重點。第一個重點是說話時要連音。所謂「連音」是指講話時將兩個不同的字連起來說，這樣聽起來就像一個字一樣，例如把 do you 說成 [duju]，或者把 I want to 說成 [aɪ] [wɑnə] 等。如果非常仔細地聽聽力 1.3 中使用 set-phrases 的方式，應該就可以聽出其他相同的發音習慣。

　　第二個重點是講電話時要注意語調，發音才會清楚。「語調」是指聲音的抑揚頓挫，也就是說話時聲調的高低。中文人士講英文時語調聽起來會很平板，給人不甚親切的感覺而不自知，這便是語調錯用之故。若希望在講電話時聽起來親切有禮，就得盡量將語調起伏的範圍拉大，比一般平常面對面談話時誇張。請聽聽力 1.3 中的 set-phrases 示範，應該也能聽出我所謂的語調。

　　練習 set-phrases 的發音時，請盡量模仿 MP3 中的連音和語調。起初可能會覺得有一點奇怪，但記住，這是由於初次練習的緣故。所以請切記這兩個重點。

Task 1.6

　　現在重新聽一遍聽力 1.1 中的電話對話，看能聽出多少個必備語庫 1.1 中的 set-phrases。注意 set-phrases 的用法。

　　接下來，我們再來看一看基本電話用語中一些常見的片語動詞 chunks。

Task 1.7

連連看。請將下面表格左欄的動詞 chunks 與右欄的例句加以配對。

動詞 chunks	例句
1. put sb. through 　幫某人轉接電話	a) Can you ask her to get back to me? It's quite urgent.
2. put sb. through to sb. 　幫某人把電話轉接給某人	b) Can you call me back in five minutes?
3. get through 　接通電話	c) Can you put me through to Susan Thornley?
4. get through to sb. 　接通某人	d) I tried to call you earlier but I couldn't get through.
5. call back 　回電	e) I'll just put you through.
6. call sb. back 　回電給某人	f) I'm trying to get through to Thomas Smith. Is he there?
7. get back to sb. 　回電給某人	g) OK, I'll call back later.

Task 1.7 ▶參考答案

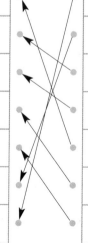

動詞 chunks	例句
1. put sb. through	a) Can you ask her to get back to me? It's quite urgent.
2. put sb. through to sb.	b) Can you call me back in five minutes?
3. get through	c) Can you put me through to Susan Thornley?
4. get through to sb.	d) I tried to call you earlier but I couldn't get through.
5. call back	e) I'll just put you through.
6. call sb. back	f) I'm trying to get through to Thomas Smith. Is he there?
7. get back to sb.	g) OK, I'll call back later.

Task 1.8

請在空格中填入正確的介系詞，完成以下句子，然後找出完整的 chunks。請見第一個句子的示範。

1. Can you call _____back_____ later?
2. I couldn't get _____ him today. I'll try again tomorrow.
3. I'll call you _____ this afternoon.
4. I'm having problems getting _____.
5. Please ask her to get _____ me as soon as she arrives at the office.
6. Please hold. Putting you _____.
7. Would you like me to put you _____ one of our sales reps?

Task 1.8 ▶參考答案

2. I couldn't get through to him today. I'll try again tomorrow.

3. I'll call you back this afternoon.

4. I'm having problems getting through.

5. Please ask her to get back to me as soon as she arrives at the office.

6. Please hold. Putting you through.

7. Would you like me to put you through to one of our sales reps?

Task 1.9

現在重新聽一遍聽力 1.1，可以邊聽邊讀書末的對照文，看看各位能聽出幾個動詞 chunks？請留意這些動詞 chunks 的用法。

▶ 會議達人基本功：字母與數字

對很多人而言，在電話留言和記錄留言時，最令人頭痛的就是遇到數字和字母了，無論是想聽清楚或記下來，或念給別人聽好讓對方記下來，都叫人不知所措。所以在本節中，我們要練習的正是這些技巧。

Task 1.10

請看以下這些縮寫。花幾分鐘把這幾個縮寫的全名寫出來。例如，在商業術語中，FOB 是指國貿條規 Incoterm 中的 Free on Broad，即出口港（裝運港）船上交貨條件的意思。

1. _____ _____ FOB _____
2. _____ NEC _____ _____
3. _____ _____ PLC
4. GDP _____ _____
5. _____ CIF _____

Task 1.11 聽力 1.4 06

現在請練習聽力 1.4，並將聽到的其他縮寫寫在各個空白欄位中。

Task 1.10 & 1.11 ▶ 參考答案

請對照下表的答案，看看你能寫出全名的有幾個？你知道 FOB 的全名，那麼其他的縮寫呢？請查出你不知道的縮寫。

1.	COD	BOT	FOB	POD
2.	MIT	NEC	NYC	FIT

3.	VAT	CAP	BKG	PLC
4.	GDP	PST	GMT	GNP
5.	EGM	CIF	DCF	PPS

為幫助各位建立聽寫字母的能力,建議各位可分幾天完成下面兩個練習。

Task 1.12

請重新聽一遍聽力 1.4 中的縮寫,將所聽到的縮寫寫在一張空白紙上,之後再利用上面的表格檢查答案。

Task 1.13

請閱讀上面表格中的縮寫,並用 MP3 播放器錄音。然後將自己的錄音和光碟中的錄音加以比對,檢驗自己所念的是否正確。

接下來,我們要練習的部分是數字。

Task 1.14 聽力 1.5 07

請聽聽力 1.5,先別參閱後面的解答,試試自己的聽力,把聽到的數字寫在下面的空格中。

1. _____	5. _____	9. _____	13. _____
2. _____	6. _____	10. _____	14. _____
3. _____	7. _____	11. _____	15. _____
4. _____	8. _____	12. _____	16. _____

Task 1.14 ▶參考答案

請利用下面的表格檢查答案，然後仔細閱讀解析。

1. 0953 124 789	5. 126 7709.007	9. 123,456.09	13. A88
2. 886 2237 6421	6. Room 602	10. 30	14. 15
3. REC. 18900	7. 0000799910	11. 13	15. 50
4. DOB 12.25.1976	8. $125,628	12. 8A	16. 666.6

數字解析

❶ 0953 124 789：

報手機號碼時最好用帶有韻律的語調，就跟 MP3 光碟片中的錄音一樣。用這種有韻律的語調，對方就會聽得比較清楚，也比較容易記錄：先報四碼，停頓，再報三碼，停頓，再報最後三碼。

❷ 886 2237 6421：

報市內電話號碼時也應用帶有韻律的語調，即先報頭四碼，停頓，再報最後四碼。

❸ REC. 18900：

這個應該滿簡單的：報數字 0 的時候可以說 "zero" 和 "oh"。此處以 "oh" 代表 0 的原因是，"zero" 這個字含有兩個對中文人士來說很難發的音：/ z / 和 / r /。所以 "oh" 反而比較容易發音。

❹ DOB 12.25.1976：

這是生日的日期，所以可用數字代表年、月、日。

❺ 126 7709.007：

學會用 "double" 和 "point" 這兩個詞來念這種有重複和小數點的數字。

❻ Room 602：

房間號碼的唸法很簡單，只要注意把數字 0 唸成 "oh"，不需唸成 "room six hundred and two"。

❼ 0000799910：

這類數字很難唸，因為不知該怎麼分段才好。我的建議是，每次都用 "double"（兩個）一詞，然後接接數字："double oh, double seven"。但是，遇到這種數字重複的時候千萬不要用 "triple"（三個）一詞。因為若線路或發音不清楚時，"triple" 聽起來就像 "three four"，容易使對方搞錯。

❽ $125,628：

數字很長的大筆金額很不容易唸。各位可由左到右開始報，按照順序每遇到一個逗號就說 "billion"、"million" 或 "thousand"。遇到以百為單位的數字，像是 628，唸成 "six hundred and twenty eight"，會比唸成 "six hundred twenty eight" 清楚。

❾ 123,456.09：

MP3 光碟片中所示範的是一種報這類數字的簡潔方式。但就數學而言，最精確的說法則是 "one hundred twenty-three thousand, four hundred fifty-six, and nine hundredths"，其中的 "and" 只是用來表示小數點。

❿ ~ ⓫ 30 和 13：

這類數字對任何人來說都不容易。通常的原則是，30 的重音放在前面，如 THIRty，而 13 的重音放在後面，如 thirTEEN。然而當英語人士講話速度很快的時候，這兩類數字尤其難以分辨。所以，如果無法很確定所聽到的是哪一個數字，就請對方再說一遍吧。

⓬ ~ ⓭ 8A 和 A88：

對中文人士而言，8 和 A 這兩個發音類似的字母和數字連在一起尤其難唸，往往會把 "eight" 後面的 / t / 音發得很輕或甚至沒發出音。如果不把 / t / 這個音清楚地發出來，聽起來就會像是字母 A，而不是數字 8 了。因此，請小心清楚地將 "eight" 最後的 / t / 發出音來。

⓮ ~ ⓯ 15 和 50：

請見 ⓾ ~ ⓫ 的解析。

⓰ 666.6：

通常唸成 "double six six"，而非 "six double six"。遇到重複三個同樣的數字時，記得先唸連續兩個同樣的數字 "double six"，再唸剩下的數字 "six"。

請過幾天後再回來做下面的練習。

Task 1.15

在紙上寫下一些你所設定的數字，錄下自己唸這些數字時的發音。過幾天之後回來聽你錄下的音，然後寫出聽到的數字，再和當初設定錄音的數字加以核對。

Task 1.15 ▶參考答案

請看你第一次和第二次寫下的兩組數字是否一樣？如果不一樣，原因何在？是否你的聽力還有待加強，還是你的唸法出了錯？請重複練習幾遍。若有朋友一起練習的話，可以互唸數字讓對方聽寫。

好啦，Unit 1 的學習就到此告一段落。請在研讀有關如何開展會議的 Unit 2 之前，回到本單元前面設下的學習目標，確認是否已完全掌握本單元的學習目標。

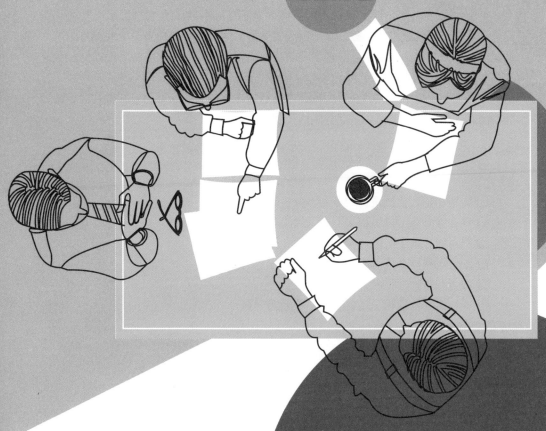

Unit 2

展開會議
Starting the Conference

引言與學習目標

　　展開電話會議往往是整個會議過程中最難掌控的階段。其間狀況層出不窮，像是：通訊一下子就斷掉；不確知參與開會的人數，所以有時難免會不小心就打斷彼此的談話；不清楚電話會議由誰主導；會議也可能很快就陷入缺乏專業的混亂狀態。或許各位還記得，我們在上個單元中學到會議小組組長的責任之一，就是負責展開會議。所以在本單元中，我們將學習展開會議的議程，以及確保電話會議順利而穩當展開的語彙，讓各位快速進入電話會議的正題。

　　在本單元的學習結束時，各位應該達成的學習目標如下：

❏ 對展開電話會議議程的各個步驟有所了解。
❏ 學會展開電話會議和表明會議目的的用語。
❏ 學會向會議中其他在場人士自我介紹的用語。
❏ 學會處理技術性溝通問題的用語。
❏ 做過許多聽力和發音練習。
❏ 學會電話會議和一般會議的一些關鍵字詞。

展開電話會議

我們就從聽一段電話會議錄音開始吧。

Task 2.1 聽力 2.1

請聽聽力 2.1 並看下面的會議議程，判斷所聽到的這場會議是依據哪一份議程？

AGENDA 1

Purpose: to help the client with some technical problems

1. Listen to the problem
2. Identify the causes
3. Suggest ways we can help
4. Establish a clear action plan for solving the problem

AGENDA 2

Purpose: to brief the client on the project status

1. Update client on points raised at the previous conference
2. Brief the client on what we've achieved so far
3. Brief the client on what still needs to be done
4. Listen to their suggestions for action points
5. Establish clear action points

Task 2.1 ▶參考答案

　　希望各位聽得出這場會議是依照第一份議程進行。如果聽不出來,請多聽幾次,同時借助本書末的對照文。

　　在這會議的初始階段中雙方組長都按照會議議程進行,確保這場電話會議能順利而有效的展開。請把自己想像成小組組長,然後仔細研究一下這份議程。這份議程共有六個步驟。

● 步驟一:

　　示意會議開始(Signal the beginning)。組長的責任包括在會議開始之前設定好相關機器設備,確定在其他小組成員到齊之前設備均正常運作並已連線。當雙方成員都到齊,其中一方的組長應該示意我方已做好準備,可以展開會議。

● 步驟二:

　　介紹小組中其他成員(Introduce the other team members)。在此時小組成員應該報上姓名。在開會初始階段介紹小組的其他成員是很重要的,並且必須請成員在報出姓名時都要清楚發音。如此要求的原因有二,首先,對方小組成員才會知道我方有多少人;第二,也可讓對方在聽到成員的聲音時能夠聯想到人名。

● 步驟三:

　　自我介紹(Introducing yourself)。報出姓名的時候應該要求發音清楚,也鼓勵小組成員清楚發音。每位小組成員在進行到步驟三時必須至少已發言過一次,如此大家才會知道會議中有多少人在場,並熟悉對方的聲音。

● 步驟四:

　　檢查連線(Check the connection)。會議開始前最好先測試連線,然後才繼續開會。在會議開始前需檢驗音效品質,確定沒有雜訊或迴聲。如果線路不清楚,此時可停止通話,重新以品質較好的線路連線。

● 步驟五：

表明會議目的（State the purpose of the meeting）。此時會議才算真正展開。

● 步驟六：

根據會議議程逐項進行討論（Go through the items on the agenda）。

現在再聽一次聽力 2.1 的會議錄音，看是否聽出是哪一份議程了。

Task 2.2

請再聽一次聽力 2.1，將下列事項正確順序的編號寫在旁邊。請見第一項示範。

Check the connection	
Go through the items on the agenda	
Introduce the other team members	
Introducing yourself	
Signal the beginning	1
State the purpose of the meeting	

Task 2.2 ▶ 參考答案

Check the connection	4
Go through the items on the agenda	6
Introduce the other team members	2
Introducing yourself	3
Signal the beginning	1
State the purpose of the meeting	5

如果覺得這個練習太難，不要擔心，一旦學會正確用語之後，做起這個練習就會簡單多了。

　　我們將繼續往下學習相關用語。在接下來的練習中，我們的學習重點放在步驟一、二、四所用到的語言。至於步驟三和五，則將留待本單元的後面再行介紹。

Task 2.3

　　請將 set-phrases 加以分類，寫在下面所屬的步驟欄位中。

Can you hear us clearly?

Can you hear us OK?

Everyone's ready here.

How's your connection?

Let me just introduce who we've got at our end.

OK, at our end we've got X and Y.

OK, here we've got X and Y.

OK, is everyone ready?

OK, shall we get going?

OK, shall we start?

OK, we've got X people at our end.

OK, we've got X people here.

OK, we've got X people on our side.

The line's bad. Let me try again.

The line's good. Let's go.

The line's ready.

We're ready at our end.

We're ready here.

You guys ready there?

Step 1
Signal the beginning

Step 2
Introduce other team members

Step 4
Check the connection

請利用下面的必備語庫核對答案。

電話和會議 *必備語庫* 2.1

Step 1 Signal the beginning

OK, shall we get going?

OK, shall we start?

You guys ready there?

We're ready here.

Everyone's ready here.

OK, is everyone ready?

We're ready at our end.

The line's ready.

Step 2 Introduce the other team members

OK, we've got X people here.

Let me just introduce who we've got at our end.

OK, we've got X people at our end.

OK, we've got X people on our side.

OK, at our end we've got X and Y.

OK, here we've got X and Y.

Step 4 Check the connection

Can you hear us clearly?

How's your connection?

The line's bad. Let me try again.

Can you hear us OK?

The line's good. Let's go.

語庫解析

● Step 1 ：
get going 是「開始」的意思，有時也有「離開」之意，不過在電話會議中永遠是「開始」的意思。

● Step 2 ：
at our end 是「到場」的意思。 On our side 也是「到場」的意思。

● Step 4 ：
如果檢查連線時線路良好，可以說： The line's good. Let's go.。如果連線很差要重新連線的話，可以說： The line's bad. Let me try again.。

　　好，現在我們來練習發音。練習發音的同時也別忘了在 Unit 1 介紹過的重點，說話時多運用連音並注意聲調。

Task 2.4 聽力 2.2　 09

　　利用聽力 2.2 練習必備語庫 2.1 中 set-phrases 的發音。.

　　我們先來研究一些在步驟二、三用來自我介紹的用語，然後再學習表明會議目的的用語。

Task 2.5 聽力 2.3

學習必備語庫 2.2 中自我介紹的用語，然後利用聽力 2.3 練習發音。

電話和會議 必備語庫 2.2

Introducing yourself

Hi there, I'm X.

Hello, this is X.

Hi, you can call me X.

Hello, my name is X.

Hello, X here.

現在來看展開會議的第五個步驟中，表明會議目的的用語。

Task 2.6 聽力 2.4

閱讀以下必備語庫 2.3 的 set-phrases 和解析，然後利用聽力 2.4 練習 set-phrases 的發音。

電話和會議 必備語庫 2.3

State the purpose of the meeting

We're having this meeting to V ....

We're having this meeting because + clause.

The purpose of this meeting is to V ....

The reason I've called this meeting is to V ....

The reason I've called this meeting is because + clause.

What we want to do today is V ....

What we need to do today is V ....

What we have to do today is V ....

語庫解析

　　雖然這些 set-phrases 都是用 meeting 一詞，電話會議還是適用。背這些 set-phrases 時請特別注意結尾部分，有的是接 clause ，有的則是接 V 。請看以下範例，這些句子的 clause 和 V 部分都畫了底線。

- The purpose of this meeting is to <u>discuss</u> the new project.
- What we want to do today is <u>talk</u> about the market situation here.
- The reason I've called this meeting is because <u>many of our clients are complaining about our products</u>.
- We're having this meeting because <u>the project deadline is coming up</u> and I want to make sure that everyone knows what to do in the next stage.

　　現在請再次聆聽聽力 2.1 中的電話會議錄音，以鞏固目前為止所學到的用語。並請看目前為止學過的 set-phrases 出現了多少次。

Task 2.7

　　請再聽一次聽力 2.1 的電話會議，將所聽到必備語庫 2.1 、 2.2 、 2.3 的 set-phrases 勾出來。

Task 2.7 ▶參考答案

　　各位可能需要重複聆聽錄音二到三遍。請先多聽幾次，盡量不要閱讀對照文，接下來再閱讀對照文，看自己是否聽出所有的 set-phrases 。請一邊聽取錄音的時候，一邊注意 set-phrases 的用法。

處理溝通問題

　　有時在開電話會議或打長途電話時可能會遇到連線上的問題，例如線路突然中斷、出現干擾音甚或訊號品質低劣。在本節中我們要學的正是處理此類問題的用語。至於語言上所引起的溝通問題，則將留待 Unit 5 再為各位詳細說明，本節的重點將先放在由機器設備所引起的溝通問題。

Task 2.8 聽力 2.5 12

請聽聽力 2.5，並回答下面問題。
- 問題出在何處？
- 他們如何解決問題？

Task 2.8 ▶參考答案

　　問題在於線路干擾，造成訊號斷斷續續。A 聽不到 B，但 B 似乎聽得到 A。於是 A 組決定再打一次電話，以重新連線。

　　現在就來學習重打一次電話時的用語。

Task 2.9

請學習下面必備語庫 2.4 的 set-phrases，然後閱讀解析。

電話和會議 必備語庫 2.4

Can you hear us?

Can you say that last bit again please? We didn't get that.

Can you slow down a bit, please?

Can you speak up a bit, please?

Can you turn up your microphone?

Hello?

I think we've lost you.

It's a bad line.

It's a bit hissy.

Let's try again.

Our connection is weak.

Sorry, I didn't catch that last bit.

Sorry, again please.

The line's not very good.

There's a bit of a delay.

There's a problem with the line.

There's an echo.

There's some static.

We can hear you, but I don't think you can hear us.

We can't hear you.

We can't hear you. Can you hear us?

We'll call you.

We're having problems hearing you here.

語庫解析

- Can you slow down a bit, please? 這是講話速度放慢一點的意思。
- Can you speak up a bit, please? 這是音量放大一點的意思。
- It's a bit hissy. 這是線路出現雜訊的意思。
- Can you turn up your microphone? 這是麥克風音量調大的意思。
- There's a bit of a delay. 這是對方聽到你的聲音時發生延誤，或者你聽到對方聲音時產生延誤。這些通訊問題經常會造成溝通上的問題。

Task 2.10 聽力 2.6

請利用聽力 2.6 練習必備語庫 2.4 中 set-phrases 的發音。

Task 2.11

現在請再聽一次聽力 2.5，把講者提到的必備語庫 2.4 中的 set-phrases 勾出來。

Task 2.11 ▶參考答案

請參閱書末所附聽力 2.5 的對照文以檢查答案，並留意 set-phrases 的用法。

好，現在來練習運用本單元學到的用語。請先閱讀下面的背景資料欄，然後做下一組練習。

背景資料

S&M 紡織品有限公司是一家位於台灣的紡織與服裝製造商，他們生產的服裝均是根據自家的設計，並使用位於中國的 S&M 工廠所生產的布料。這家公司的客戶為歐美的低價量產品牌公司，沃爾瑪是他們最大的客戶。

Task 2.12 聽力 2.7

請聽聽力 2.7 的電話會議錄音，並回答下面問題。
- 新的內衣系列有何問題？
- S&M 的行銷經理有何建議？

Task 2.12 ▶參考答案

新的內衣系列讓模特兒穿了看起來很胖，所以客戶組的買家覺得會很難推銷出去。S&M 的行銷經理建議挑選比較瘦的模特兒。註：在此 "knickers" 是英式英文，即美式英文中 "panties"（內褲）的意思。

Task 2.13

請再聽一次聽力 2.7 的電話會議錄音，看是否能夠聽出在本單元所學過之展開會議議程的每一步驟，並將聽到必備語庫中的 set-phrases 勾出來。請先不要參看對照文。

Task 2.14

請閱讀下面的電話會議對照文，然後利用本單元必備語庫中的 set-phrases 填空，每個空格中填入一個 set-phrase。

Leader A: _____? (signal the beginning)

Leader B: Um, just a minute, we're just waiting for Eduardo. Oh here he is, right, yes, _____. (signal the beginning)

Leader A: _____: (introduce other team members) Jennifer from sales, and Jack from marketing, and I'm Nancy.

Jennifer: _____ Jennifer. (introducing yourself)

Jack: _____ Jack. (introducing yourself)

Leader B: OK. _____. (introduce other team members) There's myself — my name's Ginny — and Eduardo, the country buyer.

Eduardo: _____ Eduardo. (introducing yourself)

Leader A: How's _____? (check the connection)

Leader B: Yes, _____. (check the connection)

Leader A: OK, _____ (stating the purpose) discuss the new lines for next season. It seems that your buyer is not happy with our new line of underwear. Can you tell us why?

Eduardo: Yes, it's not good enough because (XXXXXXXXX).

Leader A: Sorry Eduardo, _____? (dealing with communication problem)

Eduardo: Like this?

Leader A: That's better. _____? _____. (dealing with communication problem)

Eduardo: Yes, it makes the women look fat. We tried the knickers on several models and they all look fat. I think it will be difficult to sell. No one wants to look fat in their knickers, you know?

Jack: Mmm, that's strange. Have you tried using slimmer models?

Eduardo: Of course, you stupid (XXXXXXXXXX).

Jack: Sorry, Eduardo. _____. (dealing with communication problem)

現在來練習一下口說。請在下面的練習中一邊看著對照文一邊聆聽錄音，然後唸出在上面的練習中填入的 set-phrases。

Task 2.15 聽力 2.8 15

練習在聽力 2.8 電話會議錄音中的空白處插入 set-phrases。

Task 2.15 ▶參考答案

這個練習各位可以重複做個幾次，用 MP3 播放器錄下自己的聲音，然後播出來聆聽，以確定 set-phrases 的發音清楚而準確。各位也可以用同一類用語中的其他 set-phrases 練習替換。

會議達人基本功：關鍵 word partnerships

在本節中將爲各位介紹的是，電話會議和一般會議中五大關鍵用詞的詞彙。

Task 2.16

請學習以下這些和 position 連用的 word partnerships 以及下方的例句。並請在空白欄寫上自己造的句子。

V	adj.	N
accept	awkward	
assess	delicate	
be aware of	difficult	
be in	earlier	
clarify	embarrassing	position
discuss	present	
explain	previous	
find oneself in		
outline		
state		

● I would just like to clarify my present position on this issue.

● I find myself in an awkward position, as everyone disagrees with me.

● We need to be aware of our customer's delicate position and try to help them.

● Let me briefly state our present position.

● _____

● _____

● _____

Task 2.17

請學習這些和 question 連用的 word partnerships 以及下方的例句。並請在空白欄寫上自己造的句子。

V	adj.	N
answer	complex	
ask	crucial	
avoid	fundamental	
consider	immediate	
deal with	real	
discuss	sensitive	
examine	tricky	question
go into		
ignore		
look at		
raise		
settle		
tackle		

- The immediate question we need to deal with at this point is how to proceed.
- I think we can ignore the question of bonuses.
- We discussed the sensitive question of price increases, but we didn't reach a conclusion on it.
- Their CEO raised the crucial question of cost. I didn't know what to say to him.
- _____
- _____
- _____

Task 2.18

請學習這些和 point 連用的 word partnerships 以及下方的例句。並請在空白欄寫上自己造的句子。

V	adj.	N
agree with	controversial	
agree to differ on	crucial	
appreciate	difficult	
clarify	essential	
consider	fundamental	
develop	general	
discuss	important	point
emphasize	key	
get to	main	
make	similar	
miss		
raise		
stick to		

- Can you please stick to the point?
- I'd like to raise another essential point here.
- Another general point I'd like to make here is that we haven't had any big block-buster products for a number of years now.
- Can you get to the point? We're running out of time.
- _____
- _____
- _____

Task 2.19

請學習這些和 agenda 連用的 word partnerships 以及下方的例句。並請在空白欄寫上自己造的句子。

approve	
draft	
draw up	
go through	
include sth. on	agenda
put an item on	
remove sth. from	
stick to	
turn to the next item on the	

- Can you please stick to the agenda?

- Could you ask everyone to approve the agenda for the next meeting?

- I haven't drawn up the agenda for the next conference yet.

- Perhaps we should turn to the next item on the agenda before we run out of time.

- _____

- _____

- _____

Task 2.20

請學習這些和 minutes 連用的 word partnerships 以及下方的例句。並請在空白欄寫上自己造的句子。

accept	
circulate	
draw up	
keep	minutes
read through	
reject	
sign	
take	

- Make sure everyone signs the minutes of last week's meeting.

- Who's taking the minutes?

- Have these minutes from the last meeting been accepted? They don't look right to me.

- If you don't circulate the minutes to everyone who was at the meeting, we won't remember what was said.

- _____

- _____

- _____

Task 2.21

請在以下句子的空格中填入 position、question、point、agenda 或 minutes。

1. Before we move on we need to settle the fundamental _____ of tax. How much do we need to pay?

2. Can you outline our previous _____? I think it would help us to remember it.

3. I think we can agree to differ on the general _____.

4. June will keep the _____ because she writes really fast.

5. Let me explain the difficult _____ I'm in here.

6. Let's consider the next _____.

7. I haven't had time to read through the _____ of the previous meeting.

8. That item was removed from the _____. We don't have time to talk about it in this conference.

9. We need to discuss the next point on the _____.

10. Why didn't you include it on the _____? We can't talk about it now.

Task 2.21 ▶參考答案

請比較你寫的句子和下面的答案。

1. Before we move on we need to settle the fundamental <u>question</u> of tax. How much do we need to pay?

2. Can you outline our previous <u>position</u>? I think it would help us to remember it.

3. I think we can agree to differ on the general <u>points</u>.

4. June will keep the <u>minutes</u> because she writes really fast.

5. Let me explain the difficult <u>position</u> I'm in here.

6. Let's consider the next <u>question</u>.

7. I haven't had time to read through the <u>minutes</u> of the previous meeting.

8. That item was removed from the <u>agenda</u>. We don't have time to talk about it in this conference.

9. We need to discuss the next point on the <u>agenda</u>.

10. Why didn't you include it on the <u>agenda</u>? We can't talk about it now.

　　好，本單元的學習到此結束。請回到本單元前面看一看學習目標的清單，勾出已學會的項目並確定本單元所有的教學都已學會，然後再繼續往下學習。

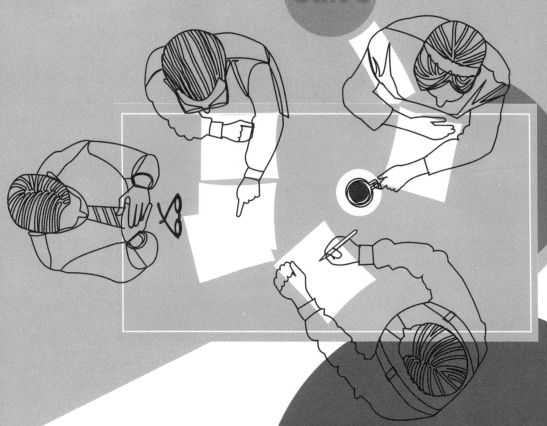

Unit 3

處理資訊
Dealing with Information

▶ 引言與學習目標

在上一單元中我們學到展開電話會議的流程，這流程在各種類型的會議中都能派上用場。在接下來的三個單元中，我們的學習將側重於三種不同類型的會議：開會重點在於交換資訊的正式和一般會議（informational conferences 資訊交流型會議——即本單元）、討論並解決問題的正式和一般會議（problem solution conferences 問題解決型會議—— Unit 4），以及討論和決定未來計畫的正式和一般會議（planning and decision-making conferences 計畫和決策型會議—— Unit 5）。

在本單元中我們的教學重點是資訊交流型會議（informational conferences）。

任何正式和一般會議都有一個重要環節，即簡報或報告最新情況，甚至一場會議中可能會有不同的小組或小組成員輪番上陣做簡報。大致上簡報可分為兩種，第一種是所謂的平行式簡報：這類簡報要報告的是狀況，與時間無關，也就是說，做這類報告描述的是情況或事實，而非隨著時間而轉變的情況，例如各位可能需要說明市場或產業的主要特徵。第二類是所謂的垂直式簡報，也就是說，這類報告描述的是隨著時間而轉變的情況，例如各位可能需要說明某個案子的進度。當然，任何簡報可能兩類報告均包含在內。我們在本單元中要學的便是用於這兩類簡報的語言。

本單元的學習結束束之前，你應該：

❑ 對平行式簡報有清楚的概念。
❑ 做平行式簡報時善於利用組織的 set-phrases，明確顯示簡報架構。
❑ 對垂直式簡報有清楚的概念。
❑ 做垂直式簡報時有能力使用 set-phrases，明確顯示簡報內容的時間順序。
❑ 能夠以有禮而恰當的用語打斷他人的話，及遏止或允許他人打斷自己的話。
❑ 能夠請他人參照你所發閱的資料和 powerpoint 幻燈片。
❑ 做過許多聽力和發音練習。
❑ 學到一些有用的語詞，可以概略或含糊地舉出某些字詞和數據。

我們這就從聆聽一段會議錄音開始學習。請先閱讀背景資料欄，然後做 Task 3.1。在聽的時候最好不要看對照文，這樣比較有利於改善聽力。如果覺得太難，可以先多聽幾次再閱讀對照文。

背景資料

攝政茶行是一家專賣高級茶葉的英國公司。他們想藉由一種叫 TipTops 的新現成茶產品將事業版圖擴大到亞洲飲茶市場，目前已選定台灣為首推市場，並和一家國際廣告公司的台灣分公司合作推銷產品。在這場電話會議中 A 組是台灣廣告公司，他們正在報告對現成茶市場的調查結果。

Task **3.1** 聽力 3.1 16

請聽聽力 3.1 並回答以下問題：

● 崔西說台灣的現成茶市場有哪些特徵？

● 崔西說這個市場中有哪類產品很受歡迎？

● 麥克說消費者調查的結果如何？

● 你能否聽出崔西和麥克的簡報有哪些不同之處？

Task 3.1 ▶參考答案

- 崔西說這類產品的主要銷售管道是便利商店和超級市場，而且台灣的便利商店爲數眾多。
- 崔西說現成茶是最受歡迎的一種飲料，接下來依序是咖啡、運動飲料、汽水和啤酒。
- 麥克說他們正在利用焦點團體（focus group）深入了解目標消費者的消費習慣，同時也正在建立目標族群的特徵。
- 崔西在開始報告之前會詢問是否每個人都聽得到她的聲音，你注意到了嗎？這個做法非常好。
- B 組的約翰會先報上名字才打斷講者的話，你注意到了嗎？這個做法也非常好。
- 崔西的報告是平行式的，你發現了嗎？她所說明的是市場的狀況和條件，而非轉變。反觀麥克的報告則是垂直式的，他是描述案子在時間上的進度。

請再聽幾次這段錄音，直到聽得出我在上面點出的一些重點爲止，但是現在還別翻閱對照文。若第一次沒能聽懂全部內容，不要擔心。

好，現在我們繼續往下學習，看一看崔西和麥克在簡報時用到的一些用語。

進行簡報

　　在本節中我們首先要學習的是平行式簡報用語。通常這類簡報是說明市場、產業或特定市場、產業的某種情況。做這類簡報時，必須清楚顯示出簡報的流程架構，聽者才比較能夠輕易跟上你的說明。做簡報時，可以用一些 set-phrases 來表示你將要開始進行簡報，也有一些 set-phrases 可以用來補充新想法或接續下一部分的說明。各位也可以用 set-phrases 為說明的項目舉出特定範例，例如數據。另外，還有對比的 set-phrases，可用於提出相反看法，或表示剛剛講的事情是例外、不能歸類在一般狀況之中。現在我們就來學習這些 set-phrases。

Task 3.2

　　請將 set-phrases 分類，在各個 set-phrase 旁邊寫上所屬的類別字母（如 B、A、I 和 C）。請參考範例所示。

B = Beginning	A = Adding	I = Illustrating	C = Contrasting
I	A case in point is n.p.		
	Also, ...		
	And another thing, ...		
	And on top of that, ...		
	Another thing, ...		
	As well as this, ...		
	Besides that, ...		
	But then again, ...		
	By way of illustration let's look at n.p.		
	By way of illustration let's look at the way that + clause.		
	Even so, ...		
	First of all, ...		
	First, ...		
	Firstly, ...		
	For example, ...		

For instance, ...

Furthermore, ...

However, ...

I just want to brief you all on n.p.

I would now like to turn briefly to n.p.

... i.e., ...

I'd like to make a few remarks about n.p.

I'd like to update you all on n.p.

In addition, ...

In spite of n.p. I still think that + clause.

Let's move on to n.p. ...

... like ...

Look at the way that + clause.

Moreover, ...

Moving on now to n.p.

Not only that, but ...

On the one hand, ..., but on the other (hand) ...

One exception to this is n.p.

... plus the fact that + clause.

Second, ...

Secondly, ...

... such as ...

Take for example n.p.

Take the way that + clause.

The next issue I would like to focus on is n.p.

Then, ...

Third, ...

Thirdly, ...

To begin, ...

To give you an idea, look at n.p.

To give you an idea, look at the way that + clause.

To give you an idea, take the way that + clause.

To give you an idea, take n.p.

To start with ...

Turning to n.p.

What's more, ...

Task **3.2** ▶參考答案

請看下面的必備語庫和解析。

電話和會議 **必備語庫 3.1**

Beginning

I'd like to make a few remarks about n.p.

I'd like to update you all on n.p.

I just want to brief you all on n.p.

First, ...

Firstly, ...

To begin, ...

To start with, ...

First of all, ...

Adding

Secondly, ...

Thirdly, ...

Second, ...

Third, ...

Also, ...

Another thing ...

As well as this, ...

Then, ...

What's more, ...

And another thing, ...

In addition, ...

Besides that, ...

And on top of that, ...

Not only that, but ...

... plus the fact that + clause.

Moreover, ...

Furthermore, ...

Turning to n.p.

Let's move on to n.p.

Moving on now to n.p.

I would now like to turn briefly to n.p.

The next issue I would like to focus on is n.p.

Illustrating

For example, ...

... i.e., ...

For instance, ...

Take the way that + clause.

Take for example n.p.

To give you an idea, take n.p.

To give you an idea, take the way that + clause.

... such as ...

To give you an idea, look at n.p.

To give you an idea, look at the way that + clause.

Look at the way that + clause.

By way of illustration let's look at n.p.

By way of illustration let's look at the way that + clause.

A case in point is n.p.

... like ...

Contrasting

However, ...

On the one hand, ..., but on the other (hand) ...

In spite of n.p. I still think that + clause.

But then again, ...

Even so, ...

One exception to this is n.p.

語庫解析

Beginning 開始：

請仔細研究這組 set-phrases，看看當中哪些是以 n.p. 結尾。

Adding 補充說明：

- 注意，你可以說 second/secondly 或 third/ thirdly，但接下來就不要繼續說 fourth/fourthly 和 fifth/fifthly 等。永遠記住，講到「第三點」之後就別再用這種方式列舉下去，從第三點之後可改用其他補充的 set-phrases，這是因為再繼續講下去，到最後搞不好連自己都忘了講到第幾點了！除此之外，英語人士每次列舉都不會超過三點，例如：This book is useful, informative, and well organized。請習慣這種方式。
- 這些 set-phrases 的排列順序都是由非正式到很正式。
- 這些 set-phrases：Turning to n.p. / Let's move on to n.p. / Moving on now to n.p. / I would now like to turn briefly to n.p. / The next issue I would like to focus on is n.p. 都可用來銜接不同段落，其他 set-phrases 則可用於同一段落中補充其他論點。
- 請注意，應該說 besides that，而非 besides。

Illustrating 說明：

注意，這裡有很多 set-phrases 都以 n.p. 結尾。如果想要加 clause，就得先在後面加上 the way that 才行。

Contrasting 對比：

> 同樣的，請注意哪些 set-phrases 用 + clause，哪些則用 n.p.。

現在來練習發音吧。

Task 3.3 聽力 3.2 17

請利用聽力 3.2 練習必備語庫 3.1 中 set-phrases 的發音。

Task 3.4

請再播放一次聽力 3.1 聽會議中崔西的簡報，把所聽到必備語庫 3.1 中的 set-phrases 勾出來。

Task 3.4 ▶參考答案

你應該聽得出來總共有兩個開場白、三個補充、一個對比 set-phrases。多做幾次練習直到全部都聽出來爲止。請注意講者如何使用這些 set-phrases 來表示簡報的架構。

好，現在我們就來練習使用這些 set-phrases。

Task 3.5

請閱讀下面的簡報，並在用來組織簡報結構的 set-phrases 下面畫線。

OK, well, I just want to brief you all on the ready-to-drink market here in Taiwan. To start with, let's look at the character of the market. The main outlet for this kind of product is convenience stores, for instance, 7-Eleven and Niko Mart. Supermarkets also carry quite a large range of these products. Even so, the main bulk of sales come from convenience stores. If you've been to Taiwan, you'll know how many convenience stores there are here — almost one on every corner. I would now like to turn briefly to the products. What kind of products are the most popular? Page five shows the range of products and their market share. You can see that bottled teas are bigger sellers compared with coffee, sport drinks, soft drinks, and beer. What's more, the market has been growing for the last two years with more local products coming onto the market. This means that the market is getting more competitive. Most of the tea products on the market are not luxury items, and also, most of them are not milk tea products.

Task 3.6

現在請練習閱讀下面的簡報，同時改用必備語庫 3.1 中同一種類的 set-phrases 取代剛才畫了線的 set-phrases。

下面是相同的簡報但 set-phrases 都替換掉了，供各位參考。另外還可以播放聽力 3.3 聽取這段簡報的錄音。

OK, well, I'd like to make a few remarks about the ready-to-drink market here in Taiwan. First of all, let's look at the character of the market. The main outlet for this kind of product is convenience stores, like 7-Eleven and Niko Mart. Supermarkets also carry quite a large range of these products. But then again, the main bulk of sales come from convenience stores. If you've been to Taiwan, you'll know how many convenience stores there are here — almost one on every corner. The next issue I would like to focus on is the products. What kind of products are the most popular? Page five shows the range of products and their market share. You can see that bottled teas are bigger sellers compared with coffee, sport drinks, soft drinks, and beer. In addition, the market has been growing for the last two years with more local products coming onto the market. This means that the market is getting more competitive. Most of the tea products on the market are not luxury items, and on top of that, most of them are not milk tea products.

Task 3.7

現在進入本階段最後一個練習。請利用在本節學到的 set-phrases 描述自己所處的市場或產業的主要特徵。用 MP3 播放器錄音，然後放出來聽聽看。想想可以如何改進？Set-phrases 都用對了嗎？然後再練習一次，看是否能夠講得更加流利。請盡量模仿 MP3 錄音中的說話方式。

我們繼續往下學習垂直式簡報吧。垂直式簡報所要說明的是事情隨著時間的進度，例如某個案子或新產品的進展。這類簡報會比平行式簡報容易組織，因為只要以時間順序當作簡報的架構，描述案子從過去、現在到未來的情況即可。舉例來說，各位可以從案子中已達成的事項講起，接著說明目前正在進行而尚未完成的事項，最後報告接下來應該完成的事項。

現在來看一看可用於這類簡報的 set-phrases 吧。

Task 3.8

請將 set-phrases 分類，在各個 set-phrase 旁邊寫上所屬的類別字母（如 C、U 和 A）。請參考範例所示。

C = describing Completed results	U = describing Uncompleted activities	A = describing Arrangements

U	... so that still needs more work.
	... so that still needs to be done.
	... so that's done.
	... so that's not ready yet.
	... we're working on it.
	Our intention is to V ...
	Our plan is to V ...
	Right now, we're in the middle of Ving ...
	We haven't managed to V ... yet.
	We haven't p.p. yet ...
	We intend to V ...
	We're (also) going to V ...
	We're in the process of Ving ...
	... we're still trying.
	We're making arrangements for n.p. ...
	We're making arrangements to V ...
	We're taking steps to V ...
	We're trying to V ...
	We're Ving ...
	We've already p.p. ...
	We've been Ving ...
	We've decided to V ...

... so that's finished.
We've just p.p. ...
We've made arrangements for n.p. ...
We've made arrangements to V ...
We've managed to V ...
We've p.p. ...
... so that's ready to go.

Task 3.8 ▶參考答案

請利用下面的必備語庫檢查答案，然後閱讀解析。

電話和會議 **必備語庫 3.2**

C = describing Completed results	U = describing Uncompleted activities	A = describing Arrangements
... so that's done.	... so that still needs more work.	Our intention is to V ...
... so that's ready to go.		Our plan is to V ...
... so that's finished.	... so that still needs to be done.	We intend to V ...
We've p.p. ...		We're (also) going to V ...
We've already p.p. ...	... so that's not ready yet.	We're making arrange-ments for n.p. ...
We've decided to V ...	... we are working on it.	
We've just p.p. ...	Right now, we're in the middle of Ving ...	We're making arrange-ments to V ...
We've managed to V ...	We haven't managed to V ... yet.	We're taking steps to V ...
		We're Ving ...
	We haven't p.p. yet ...	We've made arrangements for n.p. ...
	We're in the process of Ving ...	
	We're trying to V ...	We've made arrangements to V ...
	We've been Ving ...	
	... we're still trying.	

語庫解析

Describing completed results 描述已達成之結果：	• 請注意，這組 set-phrases 都是用現在完成式（have + p.p.）。在說明案子中已達成的項目時，都必須用現在完成式。 • ... so that's done. / ... so that's ready to go. / ... so that's finished. 請注意這些 set-phrases 都是放在句尾，如：We've sent out the invitations to the press launch, so that's done.。
Describing uncompleted activities 描述未完成之事項：	• 請注意，在說明做簡報當時仍在進行的事項時，這組 set-phrases 中有很多都是用現在進行式（be + Ving）；或在說明尚未完成的事項時，有些則是用否定現在完成式（have not + p.p.）。 • ... so that still needs more work. / ... so that's not ready yet. / ... so that still needs to be done. 這些 set-phrases 也都得放在句尾。
Describing future arrangements 描述未來之安排：	• 請注意，在描述計畫和安排好的事項時，應該要用 be going to、現在進行式（be + Ving），或 intend to、plan to 等 chunks，而不要用 will。 • 至於必備語庫 3.2 中所有其他的 set-phrases，不管是以 Ving、V 或 n.p. 結尾，都請一字不差地背起來，務求仔細。

Task 3.9 聽力 3.4

請聽聽力 3.4，練習必備語庫 3.2 中 set-phrases 的發音。

Task 3.10

請再聽一次聽力 3.1 中麥克在會議第二階段的簡報，把所聽到必備語庫 3.2 中的 set-phrases 勾出來。

Task 3.10 ▶ 參考答案

做練習時先不要翻閱本書末的對照文。如果覺得很難聽出 set-phrases，請多做幾次練習。各位應該能夠聽出三個描述已達成結果的 set-phrases、三個未完成事項的 set-phrases 和兩個未來安排的 set-phrases。

現在我們來練習實際運用這些 set-phrases 吧。

Task 3.11

請閱讀下面的簡報，找出表示案子不同階段的 set-phrases，並畫上底線。

OK, so far we've managed to commission the research house to set up focus groups with three different target consumers — young women, young men, and high school kids — and the materials for the focus sessions are complete, so that's finished. Right now, we're trying to get more information about the spending habits of these groups and we've been building a profile of the target consumer. We're also trying to identify any other possible target market segments, but that's not ready yet. We're going to commission this research from another research house to spread the work a bit. Our intention is to have the target profile ready by next week at the latest.

Task **3.11** ▶ 參考答案 聽力 3.5

以下提供的是相同的簡報，但在畫了底線的部分替換了不同的 set-phrases 作為範例。這些 set-phrases 都出現在聽力 3.5 的錄音中。

OK, so far <u>we've just</u> commissioned the research house to set up focus groups with three different target consumers — young women, young men, and high school kids — and the materials for the focus sessions are complete, <u>so that's ready to go</u>. Right now <u>we're in the process of</u> getting more information about the spending habits of these groups and <u>we're also trying to</u> build a profile of the target consumer. <u>We haven't identified</u> any other possible target market segments, but <u>we're still trying</u>. <u>We're taking steps to</u> commission this research from another research house to spread the work a bit. <u>Our plan is to</u> have the target profile ready by next week at the latest.

處理會議中斷的情況

　　做報告時往往會發生中途被人打斷或你必須打斷別人的情況，這時候極可能會因彼此文化的不同而引起誤會。一般而言，在別人還沒講完話或發表完想法時插嘴，是相當不禮貌的事。如果想打斷他人，應該等上一個人發表完或講完一句話之後再插進去，不過，即使如此，還是在打斷之前，先用 set-phrases 請求發言許可或示意有話要說，才是比較恰當的作法。在面對面的會議當中，可以很簡單的用眼神或手勢表示想要發言，然而在電話上或開電話會議這種看不到其他人的時候，就必須用一些 set-phrases 讓他人知道你要打岔了。

　　如果有人要打斷你的話，你可以選擇讓對方打岔，先回應他們的論點，然後再回到之前中斷的地方。要不然你也可以禁止對方打斷談話，讓他們等你先發表完言論或講完句子。當然，知道大家都用什麼 set-phrases 表示想要插話是非常重要的，如此你才會知道有人要打岔，也因此能夠很有禮貌地處理狀況。

　　我們就來聽這類範例吧。

Task 3.12

請再聽一次聽力 3.1，你能聽出發生了幾次插話事件？

Task 3.12 ▶ 參考答案

　　你應該聽得出來總共發生三次插話事件。首先是 B 組打斷崔西，崔西允許對方發言，但第二次 B 組又打斷她的報告時她遏止了對方。B 組也打斷麥克的談話，麥克則同意讓對方發言。

現在來看處理插話事件的用語。

Task 3.13

將下面的 set-phrases 分類，在各個 set-phrase 旁邊寫上所屬的類別字母（如 I、P、A 和 R）。請參考範例所示。

I = Interrupting	P = Preventing interruptions	A = Allowing interruptions	R = Returning to your point

R	Anyway, ...
	Can I add here that + clause?
	Can I add something?
	Can I just finish?
	Can I just point out that + clause?
	Coming back to what I was saying earlier, ...
	Excuse me for interrupting, but ...
	Excuse me?
	Well, as I was saying before I was interrupted, ...
	Going back to what I was saying before, ...
	Go ahead.
	Hang on.
	Hold on a moment.
	I don't mean to interrupt, but ...
	I'd like to add something here if I may.
	If I could just come in here.
	If I might just finish.
	In any case, ...
	Just a moment.
	Look, I'm sorry to interrupt, but ...
	May I come in here?
	May I interrupt you for a moment?
	May I?
	Oh please do.
	Please let me finish.
	So, to return to n.p. ...
	So, to return to what I was saying, ...
	Sorry to interrupt, but ...
	Sorry.

	Sure.
	To get back to what I was saying, ...
	Well, anyway, as I said before, ...
	Well, ...
	What was I saying? Oh yes.
	Where was I? Oh yes.
	Yes, of course.
	Yes.
	You've interrupted me.

Task 3.13 ▶參考答案

請利用下面的必備語庫檢查答案。

電話和會議 必備語庫 3.3

Interrupting

Sorry.

Sorry to interrupt, but ...

Look, I'm sorry to interrupt, but ...

Can I add something?

Can I add here that + clause?

Can I just point out that + clause?

Excuse me.

Excuse me for interrupting, but ...

I don't mean to interrupt, but ...

May I come in here?

May I interrupt you for a moment?

May I?

I'd like to add something here if I may.

If I could just come in here.

Preventing interruptions

Hang on.

Hold on a moment.

Just a moment.

Can I just finish?

If I might just finish.

Please let me finish.

You've interrupted me.

Allowing interruptions

Sure.

Yes.

Go ahead.

Oh, please do.

Yes, of course.

Returning to your point

Anyway, ...

Coming back to what I was saying earlier, ...

Going back to what I was saying before, ...

In any case, ...

So, to return to n.p. ...

So, to return to what I was saying, ...

To get back to what I was saying, ...

Well, anyway, as I said before, ...

Well, as I was saying before I was interrupted, ...

Well, ...

What was I saying? Oh yes.

Where was I? Oh yes.

語庫解析

- 語庫中 interrupting 和 allowing interruptions 的部分是按照 set-phrases 的正式度由上往下排列，上面的最正式、下面的最不正式。
- 由於遏止人家插話很難處理得禮貌周到，在此提供以下三種不同的 set-phraes 給各位參考。

Hang on. Hold on a moment. Just a moment.	這些都是在非正式的情況下使用，也就是在你和大家都很熟的時候才用。在非正式的情況下使用這些 set-phrases 遏止對方打岔，是不會冒犯到別人的。

Can I just finish? If I might just finish. Please let me finish.	這些可在較為正式的情況下且你不希望被人打岔時使用。

You've interrupted me.	這句可在你發表重要論點卻遇到有人持續無禮地打斷你時使用。你可以說 You've interrupted me.，如此一來，插嘴的人就會讓你先講完話。這個 set-phrase 不僅很有禮貌，同時也能以堅定的口吻讓對方知道，你認為他的行為很失禮。

好，現在我們就來練習發音吧。

Task 3.14 聽力 3.6 21

請利用聽力 3.6 練習必備語庫 3.3 中 set-phrases 的發音。

Task 3.15

請再聽一次聽力 3.1 的會議錄音，把講者用到必備語庫 3.3 的 set-phrases 勾出來。

Task 3.15 ▶參考答案

　　各位應該聽得出來打斷的 set-phrases 出現了三次，至於其他類的 set-phrases 則各出現一次。如果覺得這個練習很難，可重複多做幾次，但請先克制誘惑別翻閱書末的對照文。

　　有時遇到他人插嘴，你可以請對方參照一些你早先發閱的資料或講義，來防止他人繼續插話。在本節要學習的便是，請對方參照資料時可使用的 set-phrases 。記住，如果你為正式會議或一般會議準備了一些發閱的資料，一定要在開會之前確定每人都拿到一份，如此可讓所有與會者在開會前都有機會先行閱讀資料。

Task 3.16

　　學習必備語庫 3.4 中請對方參照資料的 set-phrases 。

電話和會議 必備語庫 3.4

If you look here, you can see n.p.

If you look at page X, you can see n.p.

If you look there, you can see n.p.

If you look at page X, you can see what I mean.

You can see this on page X.

See page X for more details on this.

Look at page X for more details on this.

Check out page X for more details on this.

Page X shows n.p.

This slide shows n.p.

I've put the details in my report on page X.

You can see my report for more details on this.

Check out my report for more details on this.

You can see that + clause.

You should be able to see that + clause

語庫解析

If you look there you can see n.p. If you look here you can see n.p.	你可以在請大家翻閱某頁的資料後,用這些 set-phrases 特別點出應該閱讀的地方。不要太過在意 there 和 here 的差別,兩者都用用看,並注意聽英語人士的用法,以了解兩者何時比較適用。
Look at slide X for more details on this. Slide X shows n.p.	如果是用 powerpoint 做簡報秀給大家看時,可在這些 set-phrases 中用 slide 一詞取代 page,來指 powerpoint 的幻燈片。

Task 3.17 聽力 3.7

請利用聽力 3.7 練習必備語庫 3.4 中 set-phrases 的發音。

Task 3.18

請再聽一次聽力 3.1 的會議錄音,看你能聽出多少個上面學過的 set-phrases。把聽到的勾出來。

Task 3.18 ▶ 參考答案

各位應該聽到崔西用了三個 set-phrases。請翻閱本書末的對照文,看她是用到哪三個 set-phrases。

好,現在我們來鞏固目前為止在本單元中所學過的知識,同時也學習如何在面對面的會議中使用這些語句。

Task 3.19 聽力 3.8 23

請閱讀下面的背景資料欄，聽聽力 3.8 中面對面會議的錄音，然後回答接下來的兩個問題。

背景資料

GoCrazy 有限公司是英國的一家旅遊公司，希望增加台灣到英國的旅客人數，尤其是發展年輕人和個人旅遊這兩個區塊。他們已經和台灣一家叫做老虎旅社的旅遊公司建立合資關係。這段錄音是 GoCrazy 的新行銷經理貝瑞·偉柏和老虎旅社的桃樂絲·王在開會。

● 通常台灣到英國的訪客是何種人？他們偏好何種旅遊方式？

● 桃樂絲計畫如何發展英國旅遊市場中的年輕人區塊？

Task 3.19 ▶參考答案

● 桃樂絲說從台灣到英國大多為四、五十歲的人，他們偏好遊覽城市和參加有導遊的大型旅行團。

● 她正和駐台灣的威爾斯與蘇格蘭發展局合作發展這些地區的觀光業。她希望透過電視和青年俱樂部打廣告。

Task 3.20

請再聽一次聽力 3.8 這個面對面會議的錄音，將所聽到本單元必備語庫中所有的 set-phrases 勾出來。

Task 3.20 ▶ 參考答案

　　各位應該聽得出來在桃樂絲報告的第一部分中有兩個開場、兩個說明和一個對比的 set-phrases，這部分的報告重點是市場特徵；第二部分是案子簡報，各位應該聽得出來有兩個已完成的結果、三個未完成事項和三個未來安排的 set-phrases。除此之外，總共發生兩次打斷、一次遏止、兩次允許插話和一次回到原先話題的 set-phrases。另外還有一個請人參考資料的 set-phrase。

如果未能全部聽出來，請多聽幾次，先不要閱讀對照文。

現在我們來看一看，各位是否能夠在面對面會議中使用這些 set-phrases。

Task 3.21

　　請閱讀下面面對面會議的對照文，然後利用本單元必備語庫中的 set-phrases 來填空，每個空格填入一個 set-phrase。

Doris:	OK, _____ (beginning) the travel market in Taiwan. _____ (beginning) generally speaking, the travel industry in Taiwan focuses mainly on tours. This segment of the industry is well developed.
Barry:	_____ (interruption) Doris, but can you tell me more about these tour groups, what kind of things they enjoy, and so on?
Doris:	_____ (allowing interruptions) Most of the time, when Taiwanese travel, they prefer to do so in large groups accompanied by a guide, who usually takes care of everything, _____ (illustrating) choosing the restaurants, the itinerary, the mode of transport, and things like that. _____ (adding) is that most travelers to the UK tend to be middle aged, around 40 to 50 or so. This age group is less adventurous, they like good hotels, and have money to spend.

They kind of prefer to stay in the cities where they feel safer. They are not into mountain climbing in Wales or anything.

Barry: _____ (interrupting) can you tell me what plans you have for growing the youth market?

Doris: _____ (preventing interruptions) I'll tell you about that in a minute. _____ (returning to your point) _____ (illustrating) the top five destinations in the UK for this kind of traveler over the last five years. _____ (referring to the material) _____ these characteristics of the market, _____ _____ (contrast) there is room for growth in the youth sector.

Barry: So how do you intend to do that?

Doris: OK, let me tell you what we've been doing. _____ (completed results) in touch with the Wales and Scottish Tourist development offices here in Taiwan and they're interested in working with us to promote their regions to the youth segment. _____ (completed results) implement an advertising campaign focusing on the excitement of the activities in those regions.

Barry: _____ (interrupting)

Doris: _____ (allowing interruptions)

Barry: How much is it going to cost, and who is going to pay?

Doris: Well, at the moment, _____ (uncompleted activities) work out those details. _____ (uncompleted activities) come up with a concrete plan yet, but _____ (uncompleted activities)

Barry: I see. OK. So what's next?

Doris: Well, _____ (future arrangements) have some features about these regions in some youth magazines. _____ (future arrangements) run some ads on TV and put some flyers in places where young people go, like the gym and student organizations. _____ (future arrangements) have some activities at big shopping malls and department stores around town.

現在我們來練習口說。在下面的練習中，請聽聽力 3.9 的錄音並閱讀前面的對照文，默唸在練習中所填入的 set-phrases。

Task 3.22 聽力 3.9

練習在以上這段會議的空白處插入 set-phrases。

Task 3.22 ▶參考答案

建議各位多做幾次這個練習，並用 MP3 播放器錄音。聽自己的錄音，確定所有的 set-phrases 發音清楚而準確。請盡量流利地説出這些 set-phrases。

會議達人基本功：概括性與語意含糊的用語

　　在本單元的最後一節當中，我們將學習概括性的用語以及語意含糊的用語。概括性用語在做平行式簡報時非常好用，如果手邊沒有確切數據時就可以語意含糊地帶過去。

Task **3.23** 聽力 3.10 **25**

　　請看下面的必備語庫 3.5 和例句，學習概括性的說法。並利用聽力 3.10 來學習發音。

電話和會議 **必備語庫 3.5**

... basically ...

... for the most part ...

... has a tendency to V ...

... on the whole ...

... roughly speaking ...

... tends to V ...

... usually ...

As a rule, ...

At a rough estimate ...

By and large, ...

Generally speaking, ...

In general, ...

In most cases, ...

In my experience, ...

Most of the time, ...

Usually, ...

- By and large, we make a loss on this kind of deal.
- This kind of deal tends to make a loss.
- In general, the market is very competitive.
- Most of the time, we receive payment on time.

Task 3.24

練習將下列句子加上一些必備語庫 3.5 的 set-phrases，造出比較概括性的句子。

- We make a loss on this kind of deal.
- This customer pays on time.
- The system works well.
- We give satisfaction.
- Cross-strait tension affects our business.
- Customs delays add 4% to the cost.
- My Internet connection is slow at this time of day.
- It's cold at this time of year.
- Most of our customers are in the U.S.
- The train is on time.
- He works late.

Task 3.24 ▶參考答案

下面提供一些造句的範例。研讀這些例句時，請注意有些 set-phrases 可以放在句首、句中或句尾。

- We make a loss on this kind of deal, as a rule.
- In my experience, this customer pays on time.
- By and large, the system works well.
- We usually give satisfaction.
- Cross-strait tension has a tendency to affect our business.
- Roughly speaking, customs delays add 4% to the cost.

- For the most part, my Internet connection is slow at this time of day.
- It's usually cold at this time of year.
- Most of our customers are in the U.S., in general.
- On the whole, the train is on time.
- Most of the time, he works late.

現在我們來學習語意含糊的用語。下面的用語可以在講到某些言詞或數字時使用，表示所講的事情是概略性的。

Task 3.25

請學習必備語庫 3.6 中語意含糊的 set-phrases 和例句。

電話和會議 必備語庫 3.6

Numbers	Words
about X	X or anything
around X	... like ...
X-odd	... sort of ...
X or so	... kind of ...
X-ish	
X or something	

- I think the returns are around 20%.
- It's about 4:30-ish, I think.
- It's kind of difficult to say.
- The market is like stagnant at the moment.
- I'm not lying or anything.

語庫解析

● 請避免過度使用 ... like ...。如果過度使用，可能會讓你聽起來像美國的高中女生。不過，倘若適度使用則可讓英文聽起來更流暢。

● Or anything 只能在句中動詞為否定時使用，並請放在句尾。

Task 3.26

請將下面句子的語意改得較為含糊。

Numbers

● There will be twenty people at the seminar.

● We need US$40,000.

● He's thirty (years old).

● I don't have the figures on me, but I think the total is 27,000.

● Can you manage 4:00?

● We need three days.

● It took three weeks.

Words

● That's going to be difficult.

● He said he was an expert.

● There are no figures.

● It's interesting.

● Can we hurry up? I'm tired.

● He was not prepared.

● They didn't want to cooperate.

Task 3.26 ▶參考答案

以下僅提供一些範例答案，尚可搭配出許多其他組合。

Numbers

- There will be around twenty people at the seminar.
- We need about US$40,000.
- He's thirty-ish.
- I don't have the figures on me, but I think the total is 27,000 or something.
- Can you manage 4:30-ish?
- We need three days or so.
- It took three odd weeks.

Words

- That's going to be kind of difficult.
- He said he was sort of an expert.
- There are no figures or anything.
- It's sort of interesting.
- Can we hurry up? I'm like tired.
- He was not prepared or anything
- They didn't want to cooperate or anything.

Task 3.27

請聽聽力 3.1 和聽力 3.8 的會議錄音，看各位可以聽出幾個直接的 set-phrases。也可再閱讀一次對照文，看看這些 set-phrases 的用法。

好，本單元的學習到此結束。請回到本單元前面的學習目標清單，確定所有學習目標都已達成之後，再繼續往下學習。

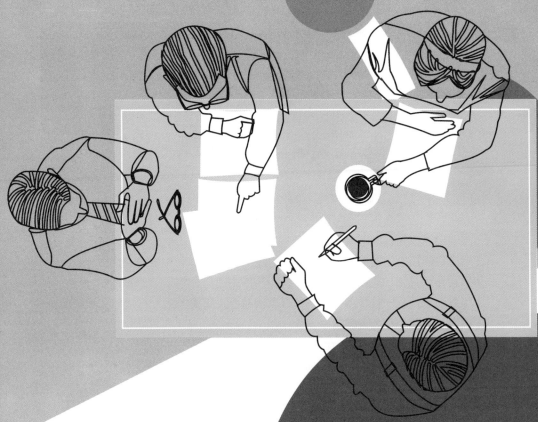

Unit 4

處理問題
**Dealing with
Problems**

引言與學習目標

　　在本單元中我們的學習重點將是問題解決型會議（Problem Solution Conferences）。首先第一部分將側重於排解技術性問題的用語。問題解決型的電話會議在資訊科技業中極為頻繁，如果你在資訊科技業工作，又必須經常幫海外客戶解決技術性問題，或者你是國際小組的一員，專門設計和建立電子設備，那麼本單元的這一部分對你來說便更加有用了。

　　進入本單元的第二部分之後，我們將側重於一般性的商業問題，尤其是提議用語，以及有禮而適切地採納或否決某項提議或建議的用語。

本單元的學習結束之前，你應該：

☐ 學會描述技術性問題並請求協助。
☐ 學會猜測技術性問題的原因並建議解決方法。
☐ 學會在正式和一般會議中提出正式和非正式商業提議。
☐ 學會在正式和一般會議中採納和有禮貌地否決商業提議。
☐ 做過很多聽力和發音練習。
☐ 知道在用 propose、recommend 和 suggest 時應避免犯下哪些錯誤。
☐ 知道在用 suggestion、recommendation 和 proposal 等詞時應該搭配哪些 word partnerships。
☐ 學會在正式和一般會議中描述商業提議的後果。

解決問題

我們就從聆聽一段疑難排解的會議錄音開始學習吧。請先閱讀背景資料欄，然後做 Task 4.1。如果覺得很難，先多聽幾次錄音再閱讀對照文，如此比較有助於加強聽力。

背景資料

橘子電腦有限公司是一家國際電腦硬體製造商，他們的總公司位於德州休士頓，總工廠則位於中國大陸。在這場會議當中，休士頓組正在和中國組討論工廠所做的一個新產品的原型，這個產品的原型有些問題。

Task 4.1 聽力 4.1 26

請聽聽力 4.1 然後回答下列問題：

● 產品原型有什麼問題？

● B 組說問題可能出在何處？

● B 組建議如何解決問題？

Task 4.1 ▶ 參考答案

● 產品原型會因溫度太高而透過電纜燒壞風扇，導致風扇故障。

● B 組說問題可能出在兩個地方：

　1) 可能是變壓器，或者

　2) 可能是主機板的設計有問題。

● B 組建議換一種變壓器，如果還是不行的話則建議重新設計主機板。

好，我們來看一看這兩組人在排解問題時用到的一些語句。排解問題時的難處在於必須將問題描述清楚，否則無法對症下藥。因此，我們就先從 A 組，也就是休士頓組所用的語句開始學習如何清楚描述問題和請求協助。

Task 4.2

　　請將 set-phrases 分類，在各個 set-phrase 旁邊寫上所屬的類別字母（如 D 和 A）。請參考範例所示。

D = Describing the problem	A = Asking for help
D 　... is giving us problems.	
... is giving us trouble.	
... doesn't work properly/very well when(ever) + clause.	
... doesn't work.	
... won't work properly/very well when(ever) + clause.	
... won't work.	
Any advice you can give would be greatly appreciated.	
Any advice?	
Any suggestions?	
Do you have any other ideas about how to solve this?	
How can we ...?	
How do we ...?	
Can you help?	
How do you ...?	
How does it ...?	
How does X work?	
Is it possible to V ...?	
It doesn't seem to V ...	
It doesn't seem to be Ving	
It seems that + clause.	
It seems to V	
It seems to have p.p.	
Please help.	
We can't V	
We can't seem to V	
We seem to be Ving	
We seem to have p.p.	
We're having problems Ving	
We're having problems with n.p.	

We're having trouble Ving...
We're having trouble with n.p. ....
What can we do?
What shall we do?

Task 4.2 ▶參考答案

請用下面的必備語庫檢查答案，並閱讀解析。

電話和會議 必備語庫 4.1 ：疑難排解 I

Describing the problem

... is giving us problems.

... is giving us trouble.

... doesn't work.

... won't work.

... doesn't work properly/very well/
when(ever) + clause.

... won't work properly/very well/
when(ever) + clause.

It doesn't seem to V ....

It doesn't seem to be Ving ....

It seems that + clause.

It seems to V ....

It seems to have p.p. ....

We can't V ....

We can't seem to V ....

We seem to be Ving ....

We seem to have p.p. ....

We're having problems Ving ....

We're having problems with n.p. ....

We're having trouble Ving ....

We're having trouble with n.p. ....

Asking for help

Any advice?

Any suggestions?

How can we ...?

How do we ...?

How do you ...?

How does it ...?

How does X work?

What can we do?

What shall we do?

Can you help?

Please help.

Is it possible to V ...?

Any advice you can give would be
greatly appreciated.

Do you have any other ideas about
how to solve this?

註：p.p.代表過去分詞

語庫解析

Describing the problem 描述問題	● 請注意，前面四個 set-phrases 都是放在句尾。例如：The mouse won't work. 。
	● It seems to V .... 不是指某個特定的時間點。例如：It seems to shut down after while. 。反觀 It seems to have p.p. .... 則是指過去發生的事。例如：It seems to have broken. 。
	● 請注意，一定要說 We're having problems Ving .... 或者 We're having problems with n.p. ....。至於 We're having problems with Ving 則是錯誤說法。
	● 請注意，應該要說 problems 和 trouble，不要說成了 troubles 或 problem。
Asking for help 請求協助	● 本欄的 set-phrases 是由上往下，從最不正式的排列到最正式的說法。
	● 當然，這些 set-phrases 中的 we 都可以用 I 替代。

現在我們來練習發音吧。

Task 4.3 聽力 4.2 27

請花一點時間，利用聽力 4.2 練習必備語庫 4.1 中 set-phrases 的發音。

Task 4.4

再聽一次聽力 4.1 的會議錄音，把所聽到必備語庫 4.1 中的 set-phrases 勾出來。

Task 4.4 ▶參考答案

　　各位應該聽得出來共有兩個描述問題（describing the problem）的 set-phrases 和兩個請求協助（asking for help）的 set-phrases。仔細聆聽這些 set-phrases 的用法，多聽幾次直到全部聽出來爲止。

好，現在我們來練習用這些 set-phrases。

Task 4.5

請利用學過的 set-phrases 描述下面的問題並請求協助。可參照第一句的範例。

1. Your monitor sometimes turns itself off while you are using your computer.

   My monitor is giving me trouble. It won't work whenever I am playing computer games. Can you help?

2. Your DVD player doesn't play your new DVD.

3. Your mouse is very slow.

4. Your keyboard doesn't work.

5. The cursor has disappeared off the screen, but everything else is working.

6. The air conditioning in your office doesn't work.

7. The paper in your printer often jams.

_____

8. Your printer is flashing a red light and doesn't work.

_____

Task 4.5 ▶參考答案 聽力 4.3

以下提供一些我建議的範例答案，這些答案在聽力 4.3 中都可以聽得到。

1. *My monitor is giving me trouble. It won't work whenever I am playing computer games. Can you help?*
2. *My DVD player doesn't work properly. It doesn't seem to be able to play my new DVD. What can I do?*
3. *I'm having trouble with my mouse. It doesn't seem to be working fast enough. How can I get it to be more responsive?*
4. *My keyboard stopped working. It seems to have broken. Any advice you can give would be greatly appreciated.*
5. *I can't seem to find my cursor. It seems to have disappeared off the screen. The hot keys are working fine. What shall I do?*
6. *The air conditioning doesn't work. We are cooking here! Please help!*
7. *The printer won't work properly whenever I put recycled paper in it. It seems to dislike recycled paper, but I have to use it — it's office policy. How do you get it to work with recycled paper?*
8. *I'm having trouble with my printer. It's flashing a red light. How do I get it to work again?*

　　既然我們已經學會了描述問題和請求協助的用語，現在就往下學習如何提供協助的用語吧。在此所要學習的 set-phrases 共分兩大類，第一類是用於猜測問題來源的 set-phrases，第二類則是建議解決問題方法的 set-phrases。

Task 4.6

請將 set-phrases 分類，在各個 set-phrase 旁邊寫上所屬的類別字母（如 G 和 S）。請參考範例所示。

G = Guessing the cause		S = Suggesting a solution
S	Check n.p.	
	... could be because of n.p.	
	... might be due to n.p.	
	You could try Ving	
	Check that + clause.	
	... may be due to n.p.	
	... you may have forgotten to V	
	... could be due to the fact that + clause.	
	Have you remembered to V ...?	
	... could be n.p.	
	... may be because of n.p.	
	Have you tried Ving ...?	
	... may be because + clause.	
	... could be due to n.p.	
	How about Ving ...?	
	... may be due to the fact that + clause.	
	What about if you V ...?	
	... might be because of n.p.	
	How about if you V ...?	
	... may be n.p.	
	... might be due to the fact that + clause.	
	Let's V	
	... might be n.p.	
	What about Ving ...?	
	... could be because + clause.	
	... you might have forgotten to V	
	Why don't you V ...?	
	Have you p.p. ...?	

Task 4.6 ▶參考答案

請利用下面的必備語庫檢查答案，然後閱讀解析。

電話和會議 必備語庫 4.2 ：疑難排解 II

Guessing the cause

... could be because of n.p.

... could be because + clause.

... could be due to n.p.

... could be due to the fact that + clause.

... could be n.p.

... may be because of n.p.

... may be because + clause.

... may be due to n.p.

... may be due to the fact that + clause.

... may be n.p.

... might be because of n.p.

... might be due to n.p.

... might be due to the fact that + clause.

... might be n.p.

... you might have forgotten to V ....

... you may have forgotten to V ....

Suggesting a solution

Check n.p.

Check that + clause.

Have you remembered to V ...?

Have you tried Ving ...?

Have you p.p. ...?

How about Ving ...?

How about if you V?

Let's V ....

What about Ving ...?

What about if you V ...?

Why don't you V ...?

You could try Ving ....

語庫解析

guessing the cause
猜測原因

- 請不要擔心這些 chunks 中的 might、may 和 could 之間有何差異，其實這三者並無太大差異。或許各位以前學過 may 或 might 是指過去發生的事，這概念其實是錯誤的。現在只須好好背下在此提供的 chunks 就好了。

- 請仔細看清楚哪些 chunks 是用 clause，哪些是用 n.p.。很多人會誤用 clause，說出 due to we have a problem 或 because of we have a problem 等話，事實上應該要用 n.p. 才對。小心別犯下這種錯誤了。

- 請注意 ... you might have forgotten to V .... 和 ... you may have forgotten to V .... 都是指過去發生的事情，例如：You may have forgotten to turn on the machine.

suggesting a solution
建議解決方案

- 請注意哪些 set-phrases 是用 V，哪些是用 Ving。

Task 4.7 聽力 4.4 29

請利用聽力 4.4，練習必備語庫 4.2 中各字串的發音。

Task 4.8

再聽一次聽力 4.1 中的會議錄音，把所聽到必備語庫 4.2 中的字串勾出來。

Task 4.8 ▶參考答案

各位應該聽得出來總共有兩個猜測原因（guessing the cause）的 set-phrases 和兩個建議解決方案（suggesting solutions）的 set-phrases。請注意這些 set-phrases 的用法。多聽幾次直到全部都聽出來為止。

好，現在我們來練習使用這些 set-phrases 吧。

 Task 4.9

請回去看 Task 4.5 所描述的問題，練習運用學過的語句為這些問題提出解決方法。可參照以下第一句的範例所示。

1. Your monitor sometimes turns itself off while you are working.
   - My monitor is giving me trouble. It won't work whenever I am playing computer games. Can you help?
   - It could be due to the fact that you are disconnecting the monitor cable when you plug in the game console. Check the cables at the back to make sure everything's connected.

Task 4.9 ▶ 參考答案 聽力 4.5

下面提供一些提出解決方案的參考範例。在聽力 4.5 中可聽到這些範例，請多加練習。

---

1. It could be due to the fact that you are disconnecting the monitor cable when you plug in the game console. Check the cables at the back to make sure everything's connected.

2. It may be due to the fact that your new DVD is a different region. Check that the DVD is region 3, or that your DVD player is a universal player.

3. It could be your mouse pad. Have you tried using a new one? Sometimes they get greasy when they get old.

4. It might be a cable loose somewhere. Why don't you check your cables at the back?

5. It may be a software glitch. You could try rebooting.

6. You might have forgotten to change the filters or get it serviced. Have you called the building engineer?

---

7. *It could be due to the fact that the paper is too old and damp. What about if you forget about recycling and just use new paper all the time?*

8. *It may be because the paper is jammed. Check that there is no paper stuck inside, and then restart the printer.*

Task 4.10

在本節最後的這個 Task 中，各位可以嘗試描述一些目前手邊正在處理的技術性問題。錄下自己的話，過幾天之後再放出來聽，練習猜測問題的原因並建議解決方法。

▶ 商業提議

在這一節中,我們要來看的是,在正式或一般會議中該如何提出比較商業性的提議和建議。其實在大部分的正式和一般會議中,各位可能必須應要求針對某些議題做出提議或建議可行的處理方式,也一定會需要評論他人的提議和建議,更可能需要用很有禮貌的方式表示反對或否決他人的建議。

我們先來聽一段會議錄音。

Task 4.11 聽力 4.6 31

請閱讀背景資料欄,並聆聽聽力 4.6 的會議錄音,然後回答下面的問題:

● 茱莉有什麼建議?
● 詹姆士對茱莉的建議有何看法?他自己有何建議?
● 瓊對詹姆士的建議有何看法?
● 杰奇有什麼建議?

背景資料

TomK 是位於台灣的一家原始設備/原始裝置製造商,專門為資訊科技業的知名品牌公司製造電腦硬體,最近他們的總裁決定推出一個自創品牌的系列產品,進攻消費者市場。龐大的行銷預算現在都已經編列好,準備要推出品牌了,但他們最大的原始裝置製造商客戶卻在最近下了一大筆訂單,訂的產品和 TomK 新的自創品牌產品非常相近。董事會的成員在這場會議中決定該如何因應這個情況。

Task 4.11 ▶參考答案

- 茱莉的建議是按照原計畫，還是推出 TomK 品牌的產品。
- 詹姆士不認同她的建議，覺得應該放棄 TomK 品牌的產品，繼續專攻核心業務。
- 瓊同意詹姆士的看法。
- 杰奇覺得他們應該向客戶「借用」一些點子應用在自創品牌的產品上，然後把品牌產品的推出日期延後。

現在我們來看看這些人在提議時使用的語句。先從正式與非正式的建議和提議用語開始學起。

Task 4.12

請學習下面必備語庫中的各項語句。

電話和會議 必備語庫 4.3

Making a proposal

Formal

My proposal here is that we V ...

I would like to suggest at this point that we V ...

My recommendation here is that we V ...

I propose that we V ...

So at this point I would like to recommend that we V ...

My suggestion would be to V ...

If I might make a suggestion, I think ...

Informal

We could V ...

We should V ...

We ought to V ...

I have an idea!

I've got a great idea!

One way would be to V ...

Perhaps we could V ...

Perhaps we should V ...

What about trying to V ...?

What if we + clause

Why don't we try Ving?

Could we V ...?

Why not V ...?

Would it be a good idea if we + clause?

語庫小叮嚀

- 請注意，通常正式的 set-phrases 都比非正式的長。
- 請注意，正式的 set-phrases 是用 suggest、suggestion、propose、proposal、recommend 和 recommendation 等詞，非正式的 set-phrases 則不會用這些詞。
- 在必備語庫 4.2 中學到的建議解決方案（suggesting a solution）的 set-phrases 在這類正式和非正式會議中都非常適用。

Task 4.13 聽力 4.7 32

請用聽力 4.7 練習必備語庫 4.3 中 set-phrases 的發音。

現在我們繼續往下學習一些關於採納提議或有禮貌地否決提議的用語。

Task 4.14

請將 set-phrases 分類，在各個 set-phrase 旁邊寫上所屬的類別字母（如 A 和 R）。請參考範例所示。

	A = Accepting	R = Rejecting
A	Absolutely!	
	Brilliant!	
	Do you really think that's a good idea?	
	Frankly, ...	
	I can see many problems in adopting this.	
	I completely agree.	
	I don't think that would work.	
	I don't think that's such a good idea at this stage.	
	I think that would do more harm than good.	
	I totally agree with this.	
	I'm afraid I can't support this idea.	
	I'm in agreement.	
	I'm not sure about that.	
	I'm not so sure that would work.	
	I'm opposed to this proposal.	
	I'm sorry, but ...	
	Indeed!	
	Marvelous!	
	Not bad.	
	That sounds feasible.	
	That's a great idea.	
	That's no good.	
	That's not going to get us anywhere.	
	This proposal has my full support.	
	To a certain extent I agree with this, but ...	
	Well, ...	
	What you're saying/suggesting is just not feasible.	
	With respect, ...	
	Yes, I like that one.	
	Yes. Good idea.	

Task 4.14 ▶參考答案

請閱讀下面的必備語庫 4.4 和解析。

電話和會議 *必備語庫* 4.4

Accepting	Rejecting
Not bad.	Well, ...
That sounds feasible.	With respect, ...
Yes. Good idea.	Frankly, ...
Yes, I like that one.	I'm sorry, but ...
Absolutely!	I'm not sure about that.
Marvelous!	I don't think that would work.
Brilliant!	I'm not so sure that would work.
Indeed!	I don't think that's such a good idea at this stage.
That's a great idea!	I think that would do more harm than good.
This proposal has my full support.	To a certain extent I agree with this, but ...
I totally agree with this.	What you're saying/suggesting is just not feasible.
I completely agree.	I'm opposed to this proposal.
I'm in agreement.	I'm afraid I can't support this idea.
	I can see many problems in adopting this.
	That's no good.
	That's not going to get us anywhere.
	Do you really think that's a good idea?

語庫解析

● Accepting 採納

Not bad.	如果你是個很酷的人，可以用語庫前段這
That sounds feasible.	四個 set-phrases。
Yes. Good idea.	
Yes, I like that one.	

Absolutely!	如果想要表現出比較熱切的態度，可以用
Marvelous!	語庫中段這五個 set-phrases。
Brilliant!	
Indeed!	
That's a great idea!	

This proposal has my full support.	如果想要態度比較中立，
I totally agree with this.	則可以使用語庫最後的這
I completely agree.	四個 set-phrases。
I'm in agreement.	

● Rejecting 否決

Well, ...	這些用語可以放在其他用語前面，緩和否決的語氣，
With respect, ...	如：Frankly, I'm not sure about that. / With respect,
Frankly, ...	I don't think that's such a good idea at this stage.。
I'm sorry, but ...	

I don't think that would work.	這些 set-phrases 可以用
I'm not so sure that would work.	來表示你同意部分提議，
I don't think that's such a good idea at this stage.	也就是說你同意提議的某
I think that would do more harm than good.	些部分，但不是全盤接
To a certain extent I agree with this, but ...	受，或者你對提議的某些
	地方還有疑慮。

> What you're saying/suggesting is just not feasible.
> I'm opposed to this proposal.
> I'm afraid I can't support this idea.
> I can see many problems in adopting this.

這些 set-phrases 可以用在堅定但有禮地否決提議。

> That's no good.
> That's not going to get us anywhere.
> Do you really think that's a good idea?

這些 set-phrases 語氣非常強硬而且不是很有禮貌，在你覺得他人的提議極度愚蠢時可搬出來使用。

Task 4.15 聽力 4.8 33

請利用聽力 4.8，練習必備語庫 4.4 中 set-phrases 的發音。

Task 4.16

現在再聽一次聽力 4.6 的會議錄音，把講者提到、剛學過的 set-phrases 勾出來。

Task 4.16 ▶參考答案

　　各位應該能夠聽出總共有八個提議的 set-phrases，其中正式與非正式的各佔一半，另外還有兩個否決的 set-phrases 以及三、四個採納的 set-phrases。這些 set-phrases 有很多出現的地方很靠近，各位可以連用兩個 set-phrases，以強調自己同意還是不同意對方的看法。如果未能全數聽出這些 set-phrases，請再聽幾次錄音直到聽出來為止。

現在就來幫助各位實際運用這些 set-phrases。

Task 4.17

請閱讀下面會議的對照文，然後利用必備語庫 4.3 和 4.4 的 set-phrases 進行填空，空格後面的括弧所提示的是該填入幾句該類的 set-phrases。

A: OK, I'd like to hear your ideas on this now. Julie, what do you think?

Julie: Well, _____ (making a proposal — 2) we stick to our plans and continue with the launch of the TomK brand. We've invested too much to walk away from it. _____ (making a proposal — 1) we announce our own brand to all our ODM customers.

A: Mmm. James?

James: _____ (rejecting — 2) At the moment most of our revenue comes from ODM and OEM. We don't know what kind of revenue our own brand will generate. It's basically a gamble. If it doesn't work and we can't sell any of our own-brand products because there's no market recognition, and at the same time we lose all our ODM customers, we'll be out of business in two months. _____ (making a proposal — 1) we drop the TomK brand and focus on our core business, aiming to be market leader.

A: Mmm. Joan?

Joan: _____ (accepting — 2) I've been against TomK brand from the start. Expenses are too high.

A: Mmm. Jackie?

Jackie: _____ (making a proposal — 2) delayed the launch of TomK brand for one year, produced our customer's products, and see what problems they have with it. Then _____ (making a proposal — 1) you know, how can I say this, "borrow" some of their ideas to make improvements to our own-brand products. _____ (making a proposal — 1) launch a better version of our own-brand products in a couple of months, say after six months? That way, we get to keep this big order, make improvements to our own-brand products without spending lots of our own money on testing and quality control, and still launch the brand, only later?

All: _____ (accepting — 3 to 5)

　　現在我們來練習口說。在接下來的練習中，請一邊聽錄音一邊閱讀對照文，然後唸出在上面的練習空格中填入的 set-phrases。

Task 4.18 聽力 4.9 34

　　練習在以上的會議中加入語庫中的 set-phrases。

Task 4.18 ▶參考答案

　　各位可以多做幾次這個練習，並用 MP3 播放器錄音。聽自己的錄音，確定 set-phrases 的發音清楚而準確。各位也可以練習替換成同一類的其他 set-phrases。

會議達人基本功：關鍵詞和描述結果

很多學生都會問我提議（proposal）和建議（suggestion）兩者之間有何分別，請看下面圖示：

通常提議比較正式，多是針對一個大型案子或問題，而通常建議比較不正式，多是針對小一點或較不那麼複雜的問題。然而就像我在上面提到的，在正式的建議 set-phrases 中，這兩者是同義的：My proposal here is that ... / My suggestion here is that ...。

在本節中我們要來看一看大家在把這兩個詞當動詞用時常犯的錯誤，以及將兩者當做名詞用時應該搭配的 word partnerships。

Task 4.19

請看下面必備語庫中的 chunks 並閱讀解析。

電話和會議 **必備語庫 4.5**

... suggest (that) you/we V ...

... recommend (that) you/we V ...

... propose (that) you/we V ...

... suggest Ving ...

... recommend Ving ...

... propose Ving ...

語庫解析

- Suggest、recommend 和 propose 後面可以接 that + clause 或接 Ving。
- 請注意，在這些動詞後面接不定詞（to V）絕對是錯誤的。即 I suggest you to V 是錯誤用法。
- 如果這類動詞的後面要用 clause 的話，clause 的主詞通常是 you（針對他人提出建議時）或 we（所提建議也包含自己時）。
- 雖然 that 可以省略，但建議各位還是每次都用比較好，如此可幫助各位記得這些動詞之後一定要接 clause。
- 在 suggest、propose 或 recommend 後面加 clause 時應該要用現在簡單式，不要用 should、have to、must、can 等助動詞，所以 I suggest you can try this 應該改成 I suggest you try this 才對。
- 如果 suggest、recommend 和 propose 後面加的是 Ving，那就表示這個建議也包含自己在內。

Task 4.20

請更正下面的句子：

1. I suggest you to continue the negotiation.

_____

2. I recommend we could try harder to increase our market share.

_____

3. I propose we should invest in a new computer system.

_____

4. He proposed we to upgrade our equipment.

_____

5. They recommended me to try the new color.

_____

6. She suggested he ought to take the day off.

_____

Task 4.20 ▶參考答案

請利用下面的句子核對答案。

> 1. *I suggest that you continue the negotiation.*
> 2. *I recommend that we try harder to increase our market share.*
> 3. *I propose that we invest in a new computer system.*
> 4. *He proposed that we upgrade our equipment.*
> 5. *They recommended that we try the new color.*
> 6. *She suggested that he take the day off.*

現在我們來學習如何把這些詞當名詞用，並了解最常用的 word partnerships 有哪些。

Task 4.21

請學習以下這些和 proposal 連用的 word partnerships 以及下方的例句。並請在空白欄寫上自己造的句子。

V	adj.	N
accept	concrete	
back	detailed	
consider	initial	
discuss	preliminary	
drop	final	
implement		
make		
oppose		proposal (for sth.)
outline		
put forward		
reject		
submit		
support		
withdraw		

- He put forward a detailed proposal for increasing revenue.

- They decided to drop the proposal. After further study they found it was not a good idea.

- Let's make a proposal and see what they say.

- _____

- _____

- _____

Task 4.22

請學習以下這些和 recommendation 連用的 word partnerships 以及下方的例句。並請在空白欄寫上自己造的句子。

V	adj.	N
accept	clear	
adopt	detailed	
be in line with	draft	
carry out	far-reaching	
come up with	firm	
consider	general	
follow	important	
implement	main	recommendation
make	official	
offer	strong	
oppose		
put forward		
reject		
review		
submit		

- The government has put forward a general recommendation. We must make sure we follow it.

- Our actions are always in line with the main recommendations.

- We studied the situation and came up with a draft recommendation.

- _____

- _____

- _____

愈忙愈要學英文 大家開會說英文

Task 4.23

請學習以下這些和 suggestion 連用的 word partnerships 以及下方的例句。並請在空白欄寫上自己造的句子。

V	adj.	N
have	constructive	
come up with	excellent	
make	practical	
offer	sensible	
put forward	impractical	
take up	ridiculous	suggestion
act on	tentative	
take sb. up on		
dismiss		
welcome		
consider		
look at		

- I've come up with a practical suggestion for this problem.

- We welcome any sensible suggestions.

- He made an excellent suggestion.

- _____

- _____

- _____

在本單元學習的正式和一般會議類型當中，往往有必要說明建議或提議的後果，例如在聽力 4.6 的會議錄音中，詹姆士說：If it doesn't work and we can't sell any of our own-brand products because there's no market recognition, and at the same time we lose all our ODM customers, we'll be out of business in two months.。

現在我們就來學習在這種情況中應該用什麼語句描述建議的後果吧。

Task 4.24

請閱讀下面的必備語庫和例句。並請在空白欄寫上自己造的句子。

電話和會議 **必備語庫 4.6**

If we do that,	... will V ...
If we V ...,	... may V ...
If we don't V ...,	... might V ...
Unless we V ...,	... could V ...
Should we V ...,	... will probably V ...
	it will have the effect of Ving ...
	it may end up Ving ...
	it's likely that + clause.
	... be likely to V ...
	there's every chance that + clause.
	there's a strong possibility of n.p/Ving ...
	there is every/no/little likelihood of n.p. ...
	there's every chance of n.p. ...
	it's possible that + clause.
	it's unlikely that + clause.
	there's a strong possibility that + clause.
	... be unlikely to V ...
	there is every/no/little likelihood that + clause.

- Should we implement this proposal, it will probably help us to gain more market share.

- If we don't come up with a firm recommendation, there's every chance that they will cut our budget for next year.

- If we act on this ridiculous suggestion, there's a strong possibility that we will go out of business before the end of the year.

- _____

- _____

- _____

語庫小叮嚀

- Should 和 if 一樣，只是聽起來比較正式。
- Unless 是 if we don't 的意思。
- 小心注意語庫右欄中以 clause、V 或 n.p 結尾的 chunks。

　　好，本單元到此結束。請回到本單元前面看一看學習目標的清單，確定所有學習目標都已達成再繼續學習下面的單元。

Unit 5

處理想法
Dealing with Ideas

▶ 引言與學習目標

在本單元中我們要學習的是計畫和決策會議中的用語。在這類型的會議當中，每個人都必須對決策過程有所貢獻，因此，在有人請問各位的看法時，一定得懂得如何適切表達，同時，各位也應該懂得詢問他人的意見、表示同意或有禮貌地反對他人的意見。此外，在本單元中我們也要學會在聽不懂他人的意思時請對方解釋，以及在發現有人誤解自己的意思時解釋本意。所以，本單元中的用語非常有用，不僅在計畫型的會議中派得上用場，其他討論計畫的會議也都適用，甚至在其他要求發表看法、表示同意或不同意以及自我解釋或要求他人解釋的情況，都非常好用。

本單元的學習結束之前，你應該：

❑ 學會以不同禮貌程度的 set-phrases 詢問他人意見和表達自己意見。
❑ 學會以不同禮貌程度的 set-phrases 表示同意或不同意他人的意見。
❑ 學會請他人解釋意思的 set-phrases。
❑ 學會解釋自己本意的 set-phrases。
❑ 學會直接卻不失禮的說話方式。
❑ 學會委婉的說話方式。
❑ 做過許多口說和聽力練習。

我們這就從聽取一段會議錄音開始學習。請先閱讀背景資料欄，然後做 Task 5.1。記住先不要閱讀後面的對照文，等我說可以看的時候再看，我們先來訓練聽力。

背景資料

Inflosys 是一家系統建立與程式設計公司，位於新竹科學工業園區。他們專門生產量身訂做的客戶關係管理（customer relationship management，以下簡稱 CRM）軟體程式，目前的客戶 Laguna 度假公司是一家五星級小型連鎖飯店，在太平洋亞洲地區共有八個據點，Inflosys 正在為他們設計 CRM 軟體。在這場電話會議中，Inflosys 的麥克斯和 Laguna 度假公司的東尼和瑪莉在討論這個 CRM 軟體中的客戶資訊欄位。

Task **5.1** 聽力 5.1 35

請聽聽力 5.1，並回答以下問題：

- Laguna 度假飯店的東尼認為這個欄位應該怎麼辦？原因為何？
- Laguna 度假飯店的瑪莉認為這個欄位應該怎麼辦？原因為何？
- Inflosys 的麥克斯有何想法？

Task **5.1** ▶參考答案

- 東尼覺得這個欄位的資料應該加上經銷商號碼和客戶地址，以方便行銷和財務部門取得所需資料。
- 瑪莉認為這個欄位的資料應該加上房間類型和上次住宿的日期，以方便房務管理小組滿足客戶需求。
- 麥克斯同意東尼的看法，他覺得在整個流程的這個步驟中，財務和行銷資訊的確比較重要。

如果沒有全部聽懂請不要擔心，再多聽幾次錄音直到聽出上面的資訊為止，目前暫且不要閱讀對照文。

好，我們來學習這兩個小組在此用到的一些語句吧。

陳述觀點

　　在本單元的第一節中，我們要學習的是與發表看法相關的用語。在開電話會議的時候，很重要的一點就是不怕發表自己的看法。和外國人工作時，他們會期望你提出個人看法，即使你的看法可能和其他所有人的不同。由於文化上的差異，許多中文人士很不習慣表達個人看法，請不要這麼認為。同時也別忘了詢問他人看法以示尊重，如此還能顯現出你對他人及討論的議題是感興趣的。

Task 5.2

　　請將 set-phrases 分類，在各個 set-phrase 旁邊寫上所屬的類別字母（如 A 或 G）。請參考範例所示。

	A = Asking for opinions	G = Giving opinions
G	As far as I can make out, ...	
	As I see it, ...	
	Can you comment on this?	
	Can you tell me what you think?	
	Can you tell me your views on n.p.	
	Do you have any ideas about this?	
	From my point of view, ...	
	I believe + clause.	
	I firmly believe + clause.	
	I reckon + clause.	
	I think + clause.	
	In my opinion, ...	
	In my view, ...	
	It seems to me that + clause.	
	My own view is that + clause.	
	My position is that + clause.	
	My view is that + clause.	
	There's no doubt in my mind that + clause.	
	To my mind, ...	

	To my way of thinking, ...
	What do you reckon?
	What do you think?
	What's your position on this?
	What's your view?
	Where do you stand on this?

Task **5.2** ▶ 參考答案

請看下面的必備語庫以及解析。

電話和會議 *必備語庫* 5.1

Asking for opinions

What do you reckon?

What do you think?

What's your view?

Do you have any ideas about this?

Can you tell me what you think?

Can you tell me your views on n.p.

What's your position on this?

Where do you stand on this?

Can you comment on this?

Giving opinions

I reckon + clause.

I think + clause.

In my opinion, ...

In my view, ...

I believe + clause.

I firmly believe + clause.

As I see it, ...

To my mind, ...

My own view is that + clause.

My view is that + clause.

My position is that + clause.

There's no doubt in my mind that + clause.

To my way of thinking, ...

From my point of view, ...

It seems to me that + clause.

As far as I can make out, ...

語庫解析

- 這些 set-phrases 是根據正式程度由上往下排列，表格最上面的最不正式，越往下面越正式。
- I think 和 I reckon 同義，不過 reckon 比較正式。

現在我們來練習發音吧。

Task 5.3 聽力 5.2

請利用聽力 5.2 練習必備語庫 5.1 中 set-phrases 的發音。

如同我在 Unit 1 所說，正確掌握每個 set-phrases 的聲調非常重要，聽起來才會自然。雖然各位可能對必備語庫中的一些 set-phrases 很熟悉，對聲調卻不見得很有概念。例如很多人會說 my OPINION，這其實是錯誤的，因為應該是 In MY opinion 才對，重音要落在 MY 這個字。（在本書中以大寫字母表示重音所在）。

一般來說這些表示看法的 set-phrases 的發音原則，就是每次重音都放在代名詞如 you、I、my 和 your 上面。

Task 5.4 聽力 5.3

請聽下面聽力 5.3 的 set-phrases 錄音，每個 set-phrases 都會唸兩次，兩次的聲調不同。請參照範例所示，在右欄中勾出正確的聲調。

	1st	2st
What do you reckon?	✓	
What do you think?		
What's your view?		
Do you have any ideas about this?		
Can you tell me what you think?		
What's your position on this?		
Where do you stand on this?		
In my opinion,		
In my view,		
My position is that		

Task 5.4 ▶參考答案

請利用下面的表格核對答案。

	1st	2st
What do you reckon?	✓	
What do you think?		✓
What's your view?	✓	
Do you have any ideas about this?		✓
Can you tell me what you think?		✓
What's your position on this?		✓
Where do you stand on this?	✓	
In my opinion,		✓
In my view,	✓	
My position is that		✓

　　既然各位對正確的發音比較有概念了，請回到 Task 5.3 再次練習這些 set-phrases 的發音。利用 MP3 錄音器把自己的發音錄下來，然後與正確版本做比較。各位的聲調是否都正確掌握了呢？

Task 5.5

請再聽一次聽力 5.1 的會議錄音，把所聽到必備語庫 5.1 的 set-phrases 勾出來。

Task 5.5 ▶參考答案

　　請多做幾次練習，直到全部都聽出來為止。各位應該會聽到兩個詢問看法和三個發表看法的 set-phrases。

好，現在我們來練習用這些 set-phrases 吧。在下面的 Task 中，請錄下自己的發音，待會兒好檢查自己 set-phrases 的發音是否正確。可以一邊聽錄音一邊閱讀對照文，但是第一次練習時最好不要看提示，以加強聽力。

Task 5.6 聽力 5.4 38

請聽聽力 5.4 中的提示並根據自己的看法作答。別擔心該同意還是不同意講者，只要說出自己的看法即可。參照以下範例所示。

1. Bus fares in your city are too high. What do you think?

　My view is that the bus fares are still quite low compared with other cities.

2. There are not enough parking spaces around the office where you work. What do you reckon?

　I believe the city government should build some parking structures to solve the problem.

3. Everyone should have more paid days leave. What's your view?

4. The government should make it easier for new companies to start up. What's your position on this?

_____

5. The government should make it harder for foreign companies to invest in this country. Do you have any ideas about this?

_____

6. Your company should provide a kindergarten for people to leave their kids. Can you tell me what you think?

_____

7. You deserve a promotion. Can you comment on this?

_____

8. You deserve a pay raise. What's your view?

_____

9. Can you tell me your views on the regulations in your industry?

_____

10. There are not enough women working in your company. Where do you stand on this?

_____

11. You deserve a big bonus this year. What do you think?

_____

現在讓我們繼續往下學習對他人的看法表示同意或反對的用語吧。

Task 5.7

請將 set-phrases 分類，在各個 set-phrase 旁邊寫上所屬的類別字母（如 A 或 D）。請參考範例所示。

A = Agreeing		D = Disagreeing
A	Absolutely.	
	I agree completely.	
	I agree in principle, but + clause.	
	I agree up to a point, but + clause.	
	I agree.	
	I can see your point, but surely + clause.	
	I disagree entirely.	
	I really can't agree with you on that.	
	I think that's right.	
	I think you're right.	
	I totally agree with you.	
	I'm afraid I disagree.	
	I guess you're right.	
	Yes, but	
	I'm afraid I don't see it like that.	
	I'm afraid I have to disagree.	
	I'm in agreement with X.	
	Indeed.	
	I suppose you're right.	
	Me too.	
	No, I don't agree.	
	Well, I'm not sure.	
	Well, that's not how I see it at all.	
	Yes, but don't you think that + clause?	
	Yes, I agree.	
	Yes, possibly, but what about ...?	
	You're absolutely right.	

Task **5.7** ▶參考答案

請利用下面的必備語庫核對答案。

電話和會議 **必備語庫 5.2**

Agreeing

Me too.

I agree.

Yes, I agree.

Absolutely.

Indeed.

I agree completely.

I think that's right.

I think you're right.

You're absolutely right.

I totally agree with you.

I'm in agreement with X.

I suppose you're right.

I guess you're right.

Disagreeing

No, I don't agree.

I disagree entirely.

Yes but, ...

I'm afraid I don't see it like that.

I'm afraid I have to disagree.

I'm afraid I disagree.

I really can't agree with you on that.

Well, I'm not sure.

Well, that's not how I see it at all.

Yes, but don't you think that + clause?

Yes, possibly, but what about ...?

I can see your point, but surely + clause.

I agree up to a point, but + clause.

I agree in principle, but + clause.

語庫解析

- 這些 set-phrases 是由上往下從最直接和非正式的 set-phrases 依序排列，越到下面越有禮貌也越委婉。
- I suppose you're right. 和 I guess you're right. 可在不情願同意對方看法時使用。
- 請注意如何有禮地表示反對對方的看法，可先表示同意對方的看法，然後以 but 接著說出相反的看法：I agree up to a point, but I think we should not rush the project.。或者可以提出疑問：Yes, possibly, but what about if we don't rush the project?。
- 請注意，I'm agree. 和 I'm not agree. 是錯誤的說法。 Agree 是動詞用法。

Task 5.8 聽力 5.5 39

請用聽力 5.5 練習必備語庫 5.2 中 set-phrases 的發音。

Task 5.9

請再聽一次聽力 5.1 中的會議錄音，把講者提到必備語庫 5.2 中 的 set-phrases 勾出來。

Task 5.9 ▶ 參考答案

如果覺得很難聽出這些 set-phrases，建議各位多做幾次練習，不過請先克制閱讀後面對照文的誘惑。各位應該聽得出聽力 5.1 中有兩個同意和兩個反對的 set-phrases。

Task 5.10 聽力 5.6

請聽聽力 5.6 中的提示並作回應，表示同意或不同意。請參見第一句的範例。

1. The city government should provide more parking spaces.

   I think that's right.

2. University education should be free for all.

3. The price of housing should be controlled by the government.

4. Everyone should get the same number of paid holidays in the year.

5. Unpaid overtime should be against the law.

6. The working day should start at 8:00 a.m. and finish by 6:00 p.m.

7. It should be illegal for people under the age of 21 to have a credit card.

8. Cigarette advertising should be banned.

9. The Internet should be controlled by the government.

10. Capital flows in and out of the country should not be controlled by the government.

11. The number of children people can have should be fixed at one per couple.

釐清論點

現在我們來練習解釋看法的相關用語。在開計畫和決策會議的時候，各位可能會遇到有些看法聽不太懂的狀況，或許是因爲語文障礙，或許是講者的聲音太小，也或許是聽得很清楚、語文也沒問題，但卻不知道講者的重點和討論內容有何關係；甚至你可能只是想要確定自己的理解無誤。同樣的，在這種時候請不要羞於開口，確定自己理解無誤比較重要。此外，在開計畫和決策會議時還可能遇到另一個問題，那就是別人沒聽懂你的意思，這時你就得解釋自己的意思，避免對方誤解。接下來我們要學習的便是這方面的用語。

Task 5.11

請將 set-phrases 分類，在各個 set-phrase 旁邊寫上所屬的類別字母（如 A 或 C）。請參考範例所示。

A = Asking for clarification	C = Clarifying

C	Basically, what I'm trying to say is ....
	Can you explain why ...?
	Correct me if I'm wrong, but ....
	Do you mean ...?
	Don't misunderstand me.
	If I said that, I didn't mean to ....
	Is that right?
	Let me put it another way.
	No, hang on, that's not what I mean.
	So basically what you're saying is ....
	So you want us to ....
	So would I be correct in saying that ...?
	So you think we should ...?
	So you're of the opinion that ...?
	That isn't quite what I meant.

That isn't quite what I said.
That's not what I said at all.
Well, put simply, ...
What do you mean by that?
What I mean is ....
What I'm saying here is ....
When you say ..., do you mean ...?
Could you go over that last point again, please? I'm afraid I didn't quite catch it.
I'm afraid there seems to have been a slight misunderstanding.

Task **5.11** ▶ 參考答案

請利用下面的必備語庫檢查答案。

電話和會議 **必備語庫 5.3**

Asking for clarification

So would I be correct in saying that ...?

When you say ..., do you mean ...?

Correct me if I'm wrong, but ....

So basically what you're saying is ....

Could you go over that last point again, please? I'm afraid I didn't quite catch it.

What do you mean by that?

Can you explain why ...?

Do you mean ...?

So you want us to ....

So you think we should ....

So you're of the opinion that ....

Is that right?

Clarifying

Well, put simply, ...

Basically, what I'm trying to say is ....

That isn't quite what I said.

That isn't quite what I meant.

I'm afraid there seems to have been a slight misunderstanding.

What I mean is ....

Let me put it another way.

What I'm saying here is ....

Don't misunderstand me.

If I said that, I didn't mean to ....

That's not what I said at all.

No, hang on, that's not what I mean.

Task **5.12** 聽力 5.7 41

請利用聽力 5.7 練習必備語庫 5.3 中 set-phrases 的發音。

Task **5.13**

請再聽一次聽力 5.1 中的會議錄音，把講者提到必備語庫 5.3 中的 set-phrases 勾出來。

Task **5.13** ▶參考答案

　　如果覺得很難聽出 set-phrases，可多做幾次練習，但請先克制閱讀後面對照文的誘惑。各位應該會聽得出三個請求解釋和三個自我解釋的 set-phrases。

好，我們來鞏固目前為止在本單元學到的知識吧。

Task **5.14**

請閱讀下面 A 和 B 組的電話會議的對照文，然後利用本單元必備語庫中的 set-phrases 填空，每個空格填入一個 set-phrase。

A-Max:	So you want the system to work like this: The name goes in the first input field, the next column is the date of the previous visit, and the third column is the room type.
B-Mary:	Yes, that sounds right.
B-Tony:	_____ (asking for clarification) the room for the previous visit or this visit?
A-Max:	Oh. Good point. Umm. _____ (clarifying) the previous visit.
B-Tony:	OK. _____ (giving opinion) we should add two more

fields after the name. One field for the address of the customer, in case there are customers with the same names, and the other field for the agent booking number from the previous visit. _____ (giving opinion) this information should go before the room type column.

A-Max: Oh. OK. Mary, _____ (asking for opinions)

B-Mary: Hmm. _____ (disagreeing) You see, _____ (giving opinions) the room information is more important than the address and booking number.

B-Tony: _____ (disagreeing) For the finance department, and the marketing department as well, it's important to know the agent booking number so that we can control the room prices and bookings more efficiently.

B-Mary: Yes, but the other information is more important for the house management team and front office.

B-Tony: But the front office wouldn't be using this field at this stage of the process. This is the pre-stay process.

A-Max: _____ (asking for clarification) that we need the system for the back office not front office. _____ (asking for clarification)

B-Tony: _____ (clarifying) We need the system for both front and back office, but at this stage of the process, the back office is going to be the main user. Mary thinks it should be front office users only.

B-Mary: No, _____ (clarifying) is that I think the front office will probably be the main users at this stage of the process. Max, _____ (asking for opinion)

A-Max: Well, to be honest, _____ (agreeing) Tony. At this stage, isn't it more likely to be the back office people using the system? If so, wouldn't it be more efficient to prioritize that kind of information first.

B-Mary: OK, _____ (agreeing)

　　現在我們來練習口說。在接下來的練習中，請邊聽錄音邊閱讀對照文，然後唸出前面練習中填空的 set-phrases。

Task 5.15 聽力 5.8 42

請利用聽力 5.8 練習在之前的電話會議中加入必備語庫 5.1 、 5.2 及 5.3 中的 set-phrases 。

Task 5.15 ▶參考答案

　　各位可以多做幾次這個練習，用 MP3 播放器錄下自己的話，然後放出來聽，確定所有 set-phrases 的發音都清楚而準確。也建議各位可用其他同一類的 set-phrases 替換，以練習使用不同的 set-phrases 。

現在我們來學習將所有學過的語句應用在面對面的會議中。

Task 5.16 聽力 5.9 43

請閱讀背景資料欄的說明，並聆聽聽力 5.9 中面對面會議的錄音，再回答下面的問題：

● 為什麼喬依斯和麥克想要延後整個案子？
● 崔西和朱里安希望怎麼做？

背景資料

OEM 有限公司是一家位於台灣的筆記型電腦和 PDA 製造商。他們都是根據客戶的設計製造硬體，也幫助客戶將產品推銷至台灣市場。他們的客戶都是知名的國際品牌。在這場會議當中， OEM 專案小組在討論客戶所給的規格問題，有些成員覺得應該暫停專案，等問題解決了再繼續進行，但其他成員覺得應該繼續執行專案的其他部分，不要拖延時間。

Task **5.16** ▶ 參考答案

- 喬依斯和麥克想要延後整個案子，因為客戶給他們的規格有錯。
- 崔西和朱里安想要繼續執行案子的其他部分，如材料、顏色與行銷計畫，以免浪費時間和金錢。而崔西則準備打電話給客戶索取正確的規格。

Task **5.17**

請再聽一次聽力 5.9 這場面對面的會議，把所聽到本單元必備語庫中所有的 set-phrases 勾出來。

Task **5.17** ▶ 參考答案

各位應該聽得出來有兩個詢問看法、兩個提出看法、兩個同意對方看法和一個反對對方看法的 set-phrases，另外還有兩個請對方解釋和兩個自我解釋的 set-phrases。

現在我們來練習在面對面會議中使用這些 set-phrases。

Task 5.18

請閱讀下面面對面會議的對照文，然後利用本單元必備語庫中的 set-phrases 填空，每個空格填入一個 set-phrase。

Joyce:	So my suggestion here is that we hold off with the project until we get more details from the client. Mike, _____ (asking for opinion)
Mike:	_____ (giving opinion) we don't have any alternative. We can't go ahead because the specs we've got don't match. We need clarification before we can proceed.
Joyce:	_____ (agreeing) Julian, _____ (asking for opinion)
Julian:	Well, I'm not sure. I know there's a problem with the specs, but to my mind there are still other things we can work on until we get clarification.
Joyce:	_____ (asking for clarification)
Julian:	_____ (clarifying) we can still prepare samples for the client, show them the color, and the materials. In any case, we don't want to delay the project if we can help it, because a delay is going to cost us, not the client.
Tracy:	_____ (agreeing) I would prefer to continue with the project. I don't think we should hold off the whole thing just because the specs are not clear. To put it bluntly, we can clear them up in thirty minutes with a phone call.
Mike:	_____ (asking for clarification) carry on and ignore the problems with the specs? To be quite frank, _____ (giving opinion) we're making a mistake if we think the specs are not important.
Tracy:	_____ (clarifying) Of course I think the specs are important, but they don't need to hold everything else up. I can call the chief engineer at the client side this afternoon and get clarification on the specs.
Mike:	Well, I think we should wait until we clear up the problems with the specs.
Julian:	_____ (disagreeing) Mike. Couldn't we still get on with the marketing plan for the project? The specs aren't going to change that much, and any marketing plan we come up with is not going to change that much if the specs change, right?

現在我們來練習口說的部分，請做下面的練習。做練習時，請一邊閱讀對照文一邊默唸在前面練習中填入的 set-phrases。

Task 5.19 聽力 5.10 44

請練習在聽力 5.10 的電話會議中加入本單元的語庫 set-phrases。

Task 5.17 ▶參考答案

　　如同前面所做的練習，請多做幾次練習，並用 MP3 播放器錄下自己的話，然後放出來聽，確定所有的 set-phrases 都發音清楚而準確。

▶ 會議達人基本功：委婉與直接

在本單元的最後一節當中，我們將要學習委婉和直接卻不失禮的用語。現在先從委婉用語開始學起吧。

有時在電話會議或面對面會議當中，可能必須和比較重要的人物如老闆或消費者講話，這時就得使用委婉的用語。遇到需要委婉表達的時候，只要改變句子的文法就好了，非常簡單。下面的練習將要介紹的是委婉的評語和建議用語。

Task 5.20

請學習以下這些語氣委婉的語詞和句型。

電話和會議 必備語庫 5.4

Statements	Suggestions
... would ... ... not (a) very (pos. adj.) noun.	Wouldn't ... be more adj.? Would ... be more adj.? Wouldn't ...? Couldn't ...? Shouldn't ...?

註：pos. adj.（positive adjective）指肯定形容詞，例如 good、efficient、viable 等。

語庫解析

● Statements 評語

It's difficult to do this so quickly.	由此各位應該看得出來，和以動
It would be difficult to do this so quickly. *(indirect)*	詞現在簡單式相比，用 would + V 的評語比較委婉。

It's a bad idea.	用肯定形容詞取代否定形容詞，
It's not a very good idea. (indirect)	並在前面加上 not very 之後，否 定的評語便會變得委婉些。

● Suggestions 建議

Wednesday is convenient for me.	由此各位應該看得出來，若把肯
Would Wednesday be more convenient? *(indirect)*	定的建議改成疑問句，聽起來便 會委婉一些。若再改成否定問
Wouldn't Wednesday be more conven-ient? (even more indirect)	題，就又更加委婉了。 這是一 個小秘訣，因為用這種方法時對
Could they get it done earlier, do you think?	方就非得做決定不可。要是所做
Couldn't they get it done earlier? (indirect)	決定很差的話也不能夠怪你，因
They should try to finish before then.	為這決定不是你做的。
Shouldn't they try to finish before then? *(indirect)*	

Task 5.21

現在請把下面口氣直接的句子改寫得委婉一點。

Statements

This is a stupid idea.

I prefer to meet as soon as possible.

We expect the project to be finished on time.

Doing it this way has definite advantages.

The financing is badly organized.

The project was badly implemented.

We hope you are able to complete it soon.

The client is unhappy with our service.

The system is inefficient.

Suggestions

Next week is better.

They can do it themselves.

We can cancel anytime.

They should lower their offer.

We can contribute some of the investment ourselves.

We need another meeting with them.

Why don't we try it this way?

Task 5.21 ▶參考答案 聽力 5.11 45

以下提供一些建議答案。各位可以利用聽力 5.11 練習發音。

Statements

This is a stupid idea.

This is not a very sensible idea.

I prefer to meet as soon as possible.

I would prefer to meet as soon as possible.

We expect the project to be finished on time.

We would expect the project to be finished on time.

Doing it this way has definite advantages.

Doing it this way would have definite advantages.

The financing is badly organized.

The financing is not very well organized.

The project was badly implemented.

The project was not very well implemented.

We hope you are able to complete it soon.

We hope you would be able to complete it soon.

The client is unhappy with our service.

The client is not very happy with our service.

The system is inefficient.

The system is not very efficient.

Suggestions	Next week is better.
	Next week would be more convenient.
	They can do it themselves.
	Couldn't they do it themselves?
	We can cancel anytime.
	Couldn't we cancel anytime?
	They should lower their offer.
	Shouldn't they lower their offer?
	We can contribute some of the investment ourselves.
	Couldn't we contribute some of the investment ourselves?
	We need another meeting with them.
	Wouldn't it be better to have another meeting with them?
	Why don't we try it this way?
	Couldn't we try it this way?

　　現在來學習有禮貌的直接用語。有時在電話會議或面對面會議當中必須很直接地表達。遇到這種時候，建議各位在語氣直接的評語前面放一個 set-phrase，讓聽者知道雖然你的態度很直接，卻仍不失尊重。這一招往往很管用。

Task 5.22 聽力 5.12 46

　　請看下面必備語庫 5.5 中表示態度直接的 set-phrases。並利用聽力 5.12 練習發音。

電話和會議 *必備語庫* **5.5**

Frankly, ...
To put it bluntly, ...
Well, to be honest, ...
With respect, ...
I'm sorry, but ....
I'm afraid ....
To be quite frank, ...

- 這些 set-phrases 可以放在任何肯定或否定的評語或問句前面。
- I'm afraid 不能用在問句中。

Task 5.23

請練習將必備語庫 5.5 中的 set-phrases 加在下面語氣直接的句子前面。

1. That's not right.

_____

2. No, I don't agree.

_____

3. We must try to get it finished earlier.

_____

4. Why can't you understand this?

_____

5. Did you actually read my report?

_____

6. They are not cooperating.

_____

7. I can't do this alone.

_____

Task 5.23 ▶參考答案

　　以下提供一些範例。當然，各位的答案可能不盡相同，那也沒有關係。造出自己的句子可以幫助各位記住這些 set-phrases 的用法。

- *Frankly, that's not right.*
- *To put it bluntly, no, I don't agree.*
- *Well, to be honest, we must try to get it finished earlier.*
- *With respect, why can't you understand this?*
- *I'm sorry, but did you actually read my report?*
- *I'm afraid they are not cooperating.*
- *To be quite frank, I can't do this alone.*

Task 5.24

　　請聽聽力 5.1 和 5.9 的會議錄音，看能聽出多少語氣直接的 set-phrases。並請再閱讀一次對照文，以研究這些 set-phrases 的用法。

　　好，本單元的學習到此結束。請回到本單元前面看一看學習目標的清單，確定所有學習目標都已達成再繼續學習下面的單元。

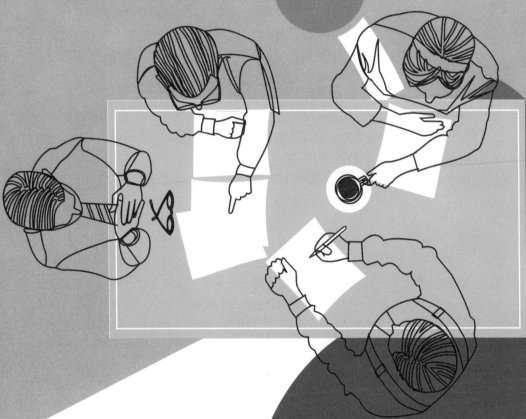

主持會議
Chairing the Meeting

引言與學習目標

在 Unit 1 中我們談過電話會議中小組組長的角色,在 Unit 2 中我們研究過小組組長用來展開會議的語句,而在本書這最後一個單元中,我們則要深入學習整個會議過程中會用到的技巧和語句。在此所介紹的知識大部分也都可以用於主持面對面的會議。

在正式或一般會議中,一個稱職的組長或主持人,在態度上應該是容許其他人表達自己看法,而不該過度強勢。如果各位有機會擔任會議小組組長或主持人的話,請務必在必要時刻才開口表達自己的看法。一場會議會淪為一言堂,往往都是因為主持人話講個不停,沒有人能夠插得上話,或者因為礙於對方是主持人而沒有勇氣請對方住口!

因此,小組組長或主持人有效處理正式或一般會議的技巧,可以區分為兩大類:處理人際關係的技巧與組織架構的技巧。主持人必須懂得處理人際關係,例如:確定每個人都有機會發言、請適當的人員回答問題、分配責任,以及確定行動計畫都會有人員負責追蹤等。主持人也應該懂得組織正式或一般會議的架構,例如:重述討論要點、確認重要項目、清楚確立行動計畫,以及繼續討論議程中的下一個議題。唯有透過確實而專業的能力,發揮技巧安排會議的架構,才能有效掌握開會時間,確定會議如期完畢。

本單元的學習結束之前,你應該:

☐ 學會主導電話會議或主持面對面會議的必要技巧與用語。
☐ 學會邀請人員參與討論和分配責任執行行動計畫的用語。
☐ 學會依據流程按照步驟進行議程。
☐ 學會重述討論要點、確認大家一致同意要點、確立行動計畫和繼續討論下一議題的用語。
☐ 做過許多聽力和發音練習。
☐ 學會強調特定事情的用語,以及一些含有 will 的實用 set-phrases。

現在我們就從聆聽一段會議錄音學起。請先閱讀背景資料欄，然後接著做下面的聽力練習。

背景資料

Fairweather 硬體有限公司是一家位於歐洲的電腦硬體製造商。他們的產品都是由台灣的一家原始設計製造商（original design manufacturer，以下簡稱 ODM）所生產。這兩家公司正在合作製造新產品，目前進行到最初的設計階段。在這次的會議當中，雙方小組正就新產品的一些規格問題進行討論。

Task 6.1 聽力 6.1 47

請聽聽力 6.1 並回答以下問題：

● A 組的組長重述了討論要點。他提到哪些要點？
● 辛蒂有何看法？
● A 組要負責執行什麼行動？
● B 組要負責執行什麼行動？

Task 6.1 ▶參考答案

● 台灣組發現 Fairweather 給的新產品規格不符合歐洲的安全規定，也就是說規格和設計都需要翻新。
● 辛蒂希望確定雙方的歐洲安全規定版本相互吻合，也就是說 Fairweather 和台灣 ODM 的安全規定都一樣。
● B 組將把自己使用的安全規定寄給 A 組。
● A 組將在研讀 B 組的安全規定之後研究出新的規格。

人際技巧

現在我們從人際技巧開始學起。在正式或一般會議中，小組組長或主持人的責任是確定大家都有機會發言，並且按照會中決定的行動計畫分配責任。我們來看一看用於此時的語句。

Task 6.2

請將 set-phrases 分類，在各個 set-phrase 旁邊寫上所屬的類別字母（如 B 或 A）。請參考範例所示。

	B = Bringing someone in	A = Allocating responsibility
B	At this point I'd like to bring in X.	
	At this stage I'd like to call on X to brief us on n.p.	
	Can someone volunteer to take this on?	
	I think X would like to say something.	
	I'd like to call on X to answer that.	
	I'd like to invite X to present his/her views.	
	I'm going to ask X to be responsible for Ving, and Y to V	
	Perhaps X would like to answer that?	
	What are your views, X?	
	Would anyone like to oversee this project?	
	X, can you be in charge of this, please?	
	X, can you find out and get back to us?	
	X, can you take care of this?	
	X, could you make sure about this?	
	X, could you please be responsible for that?	
	X, do you have something to say at this point?	
	X, I'd like to ask you to take this on.	
	X, I'd like to put you in charge of this.	
	X, will you be able to handle this?	
	X, would you care to comment?	
	X, would you like to come in here?	
	Yes, X, please go ahead.	

Task 6.2 ▶參考答案

請閱讀下面的必備語庫和解析。

電話和會議 **必備語庫 6.1**

Bringing someone in

At this point I'd like to bring in X.

I think X would like to say something.

Yes, X, please go ahead.

X, do you have something to say at this point?

What are your views, X?

Perhaps X would like to answer that?

At this stage I'd like to call on X to brief us on n.p.

I'd like to invite X to present his/her views.

X, would you like to come in here?

X, would you care to comment?

I'd like to call on X to answer that.

Allocating responsibility

Would anyone like to oversee this project?

Can someone volunteer to take this on?

X, could you please be responsible for that?

X, I'd like to ask you to take this on.

X, could you make sure about this?

X, will you be able to handle this?

I'm going to ask X to be responsible for Ving, and Y to V ....

X, can you find out and get back to us?

X, can you be in charge of this, please?

X, I'd like to put you in charge of this.

X, can you take care of this?

愈忙愈要學英文 大家開會說英文

語庫解析

Bringing someone in 讓某人參與

X, would you like to come in here? 中的 come in 是參與討論的意思，不是進入房間的意思！在講這個 set-phrase 的時候，重音應該放在 in 上面。

Allocating responsibility 分配責任

前面兩個 set-phrases 在徵求人員自願負責時很有用，然而為了節省時間，通常還是直接分配責任會比徵求自願負責者來得有效率。

Task 6.3 聽力 6.2　 48

請利用聽力 6.2，練習必備語庫 6.1 中 set-phrases 的發音。

Task 6.4

請再聽一次聽力 6.1 的會議錄音，並將所聽到必備語庫 6.1 中的 set-phrases 勾出來。

Task 6.4 ▶參考答案

各位應該聽得出來，這場會議中有一個請人員參與討論的 set-phrase 和一個分配責任的 set-phrase。

組織架構技巧

現在我們繼續往下學習組織架構的技巧。在正式和一般會議當中，需要發揮組織架構技巧的時候，通常都是在從議程的一項議題進行到下一項議題之時。以下提供一套包含各個步驟的流程，讓各位更有效率地進行到下一議題。

● 步驟一：

重述要點（Summarize）。這大概是整個流程中最困難的一個步驟了，因為你必須仔細聆聽其他講者說了什麼話，記牢他們所說的重點，然後將要點概述給大家聽。如果可以做筆記的話，這件差事可就輕鬆得多了！重述要點之時，不需重覆每個人在討論中說過每一句話，只要講出大家最後同意的事項或達成的決定即可。你也可以用中文做筆記。

● 步驟二：

確認要點（Confirm）。這個步驟是緊跟在重述要點之後。記住，在重述要點之後，一定要看在目前討論階段中所有其他的人都同意你所重述的要點沒有錯，並且同意所達成的決定。

● 步驟三：

確立行動計畫（Establish the action points）。記住，行動計畫必須包括三個 wh-：who is going to do what by when。請利用你在上一節學會的 set-phrases 分配責任。

● 步驟四：

繼續往下討論（Move on）。一旦分配好執行計畫的責任，大家都知道誰該負責什麼事情，並且事情在何時該完成，接下來便可繼續討論議程中的下一個議題了。

Task 6.5

　　請再聽一次聽力 6.1 的會議錄音，並看以下流程中的各個步驟，然後將所聽到的步驟名稱連到正確的順序。請見範例所示。

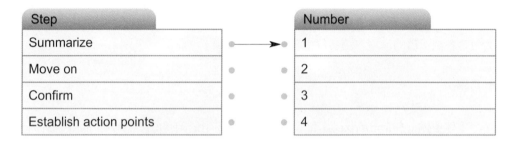

Task 6.5　▶參考答案

　　請看下面的表格核對各步驟的正確順序。

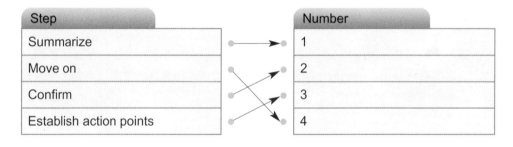

　　如果各位覺得這個練習有一點難，別擔心。一旦學過相關的用語之後，這個練習就會變得簡單。

　　現在我們來看一看用於這種情況的語句。

Task 6.6

　　將下面的 set-phrases 分類，在各個 set-phrase 旁邊寫上所屬的類別字母（如 S、C、E 和 M）。請參考範例所示。

S = Summarizing	C = Confirming	E = Establishing action points	M = Moving on

M	Any other points on that? OK, let's turn to the next item.
	Are we all OK with this?
	At this stage I think we need to move on to the next item on the agenda.
	Briefly, the main points that have been made are ....
	Briefly, ...
	Can we move on to the next point, please?
	Does anyone else have anything to say on this before we move on?
	If I may just go over the main points raised so far.
	In short, ...
	Is this clear at your end?
	Is that correct?
	Is that OK with you?
	Is that right?
	Let's move on, can we?
	OK, I'd like to move on to the next point on the agenda now.
	OK, let me just go through the main points again.
	OK, next we need to discuss n.p.
	OK, so if I could just confirm our understanding of this.
	OK, that's that. Now, moving on, ...
	OK, the next question we need to look at is n.p.
	OK, we'll V ....
	So, are we all agreed that + clause?
	So, can I just check that + clause?
	So, can I just confirm that + clause?
	So, can I just make sure we are all OK with this?
	To confirm, I think we are in agreement on n.p.
	To confirm, I think we are in agreement on the fact that + clause.
	To sum up, ...
	To summarize, ...
	We'll handle it at our end.
	We'll sort that out.
	We'll take care of n.p., and you'll take care of n.p.
	We'll take the lead here.
	Well, if I could just sum up the discussion at this point.
	X will be in charge of n.p.

Task 6.6 ▶參考答案

請利用以下的必備語庫 6.2 核對答案，並閱讀解析。

電話和會議 **必備語庫 6.2**

Summarizing

Briefly, ...

In short, ...

To sum up, ...

To summarize, ...

OK, let me just go through the main points again.

Well, if I could just sum up the discussion at this point.

Briefly, the main points that have been made are, ...

If I may just go over the main points raised so far.

Confirming

OK, so if I could just confirm our understanding of this.

So, are we all agreed that + clause?

So, can I just check that + clause?

So, can I just confirm that + clause?

So, can I just make sure we are all OK with this?

Is that correct?

Is that right?

Is that OK with you?

Are we all OK with this?

So, are we all agreed that + clause?

Is this clear at your end?

To confirm, I think we are in agreement on n.p.

To confirm, I think we are in agreement on the fact that + clause.

Establishing action points

OK, we'll V ....

We'll handle it at our end.

We'll sort that out.

We'll take care of n.p., and you'll take care of n.p.

We'll take the lead here.

X will be in charge of n.p.

Moving on

OK, next we need to discuss n.p.

OK, the next question we need to look at is n.p.

OK, that's that. Now, moving on, ...

OK, I'd like to move on to the next point on the agenda now.

Let's move on, can we?

Any other points on that? OK, let's turn to the next item.

Can we move on to the next point, please?

At this stage I think we need to move on to the next item on the agenda.

Can we move on to the next point, please?

Does anyone else have anything to say on this before we move on?

語庫解析

Summarizing 重述要點

這類 set-phrases 是從較不正式的依序排下來。

Confirming 確認要點

確認要點時可連用兩個以上的 set-phrases。例如：OK, so if I could just confirm our understanding of this. We are going to do this and you are going to do that. Is that OK with you?。

Establishing action points 確立行動計畫

請在發音時注意，這些 set-phrases 大部分都是用 we'll 而非 we will。在本單元的下一節將會介紹含 will 的 set-phrases。

Moving on 繼續往下討論

這類 set-phrases 是從較不正式的依排列下來。

Task 6.7 聽力 6.3 49

請利用聽力 6.3，練習必備語庫 6.2 中 set-phrases 的發音。

Task 6.8

請再聽一次聽力 6.1 的會議錄音，並將所聽到必備語庫 6.2 中的 set-phrases 勾出來。

Task 6.8 ▶參考答案

　　各位應該聽得出來重述和確認要點 set-phrases 都各出現一次，另外還有四個確立行動計畫的 set-phrases 和一個繼續往下討論下一議題的 set-phrase。如果沒有聽出所有的 set-phrases，請多聽幾次直到全部聽出來為止。

　　好，現在我們來實際運用在本單元目前為止所學到的語彙，同時學習如何將這些語彙應用在面對面的會議中。請閱讀下面幾組練習的背景資料。

背景資料

Chibaole Foods 是一家零食製造商，專門製造小甜品和糖果。他們最新的產品 Sickyfingers 在市場上的表現不甚理想。因此在這場會議中，管理小組正就可能的原因以及解決辦法進行討論。

Task **6.9** 聽力 6.4

請聽聽力 6.4 的會議錄音，並回答下面問題。

● 他們將如何解決問題？
● 莫里斯提出什麼樣的新建議？
● 瑪莉確立了哪些行動計畫？
● 這些計畫由誰負責執行？

Task **6.9** ▶參考答案

　　他們一開始時是決定更換產品的材料，藉此改變產品的口味和讓產品健康一些。然後莫里斯建議改變產品定位、商標和名稱，把產品等級提升為精品，這樣會比改變產品本身省錢。而瑪莉確立了兩項行動計畫：一是以新的名稱和行銷手法重新定位產品，交由莫里斯負責構想，二是維持已有的商標但修改產品的材料，則交由東尼負責監督。

Task **6.10**

　　請再聽一次聽力 6.4 的會議錄音，看是否能夠聽出本單元中所學到的繼續往下討論（Moving on）的步驟。並將聽到必備語庫 6.1、6.2 中的 set-phrases 勾出來。先暫且不要閱讀對照文。

Task **6.11**

　　閱讀下面的會議對照文，然後利用本單元必備語庫的 set-phrases 填空，每個空格填入一個 set-phrase。

Mary:	OK. _____ (summarizing) that most people think the reason for the low product performance is that the product doesn't taste good, and that our competitor's products are healthier. We need to make some modifications to the taste and add some healthier ingredients. _____ (confirming)
Others:	That's correct. / Yes. / Sounds good.
Mary:	Just a minute. Morris, _____ (bringing someone in)
Morris:	Yes, it's just occurred to me that there might be other reasons why the product didn't perform so well, particularly the pricing strategy. Perhaps people think it's too cheap. What about positioning it as a luxury product? In fact, that might be cheaper than modifying the ingredients and taste.
Others:	Good idea. / Why don't we try that? / Sounds good to me.
Mary:	OK, _____ (establishing action points) two things. Let's reposition the brand with new marketing and a new name. Morris, _____ (allocating responsibility)
Morris:	Sure.
Mary:	Secondly, let's keep the branding that we've got and modify the product. _____ (allocating responsibility)
Tony:	I'll do it.
Mary:	Great. We'll meet again in one month to try the new product and to see the new marketing strategy. OK, _____ (moving on)

　　現在我們來練習口說部分。在下面的練習中,請邊聽錄音邊看對照文,然後唸出在上面練習的空格中填入的 set-phrases。

Task 6.12 聽力 6.5 51

現在請聽聽力 6.5，練習在以上的會議中加入必備語庫 6.1 和 6.2 的 set-phrases。

Task 6.12 ▶參考答案

　　建議各位練習用同一類中其他的 set-phrases 做替換。也可以多做幾次這個練習，並利用 MP3 播放器錄音，然後放出來聽，以確定所有 set-phrases 的發音都清楚準確。

 　會議達人基本功：強調特定看法與含 will 的 set-phrases

在本節中我們要學的是強調特定事情的用語。

Task 6.13

請研讀下面的必備語庫和例句。

電話和會議 必備語庫 6.3

... actually ...

... especially ...

... particularly ...

... primarily ...

... principally ...

... specifically ...

The fact of the matter is that + clause.

The truth of the matter is that + clause.

In fact, ...

Actually, ...

In reality, ...

In particular, ...

- The fact of the matter is that we make a loss on this kind of deal.

- In particular, customs delays add four percent to the cost.

- We usually make a loss, especially on this kind of deal.

- Customs delays add to the cost, specifically four percent.

語庫小叮嚀

- 若強調某事，可在句子或子句中任何一處放入語庫前半段的單字語詞。
- 若要強調某個資訊，通常可在資訊的前面先接語庫後半段的 set-phrases。

Task 6.14

請利用學過的 set-phrases 來強調下面的句子。可參照第一句範例的造句法。

1. Cross-strait tension affects our business.

   The fact of the matter is that cross-strait tension affects our business.

2. Customs delays add four percent to the cost.

   _____

3. He works late.

   _____

4. It's cold at this time of year.

   _____

5. Most of our customers are in the U.S.

   _____

6. My Internet connection is slow at this time of day.

   _____

7. The system works well.

   _____

8. We sell this product to Europeans.

   _____

9. The product sells in the U.S.

_____

10. This market is not so profitable.

_____

11. I warned them about this.

_____

Task 6.14 ▶參考答案

以下提供一些建議的參考答案。

1. *The fact of the matter is that cross-strait tension affects our business.*
2. *In particular, customs delays add four percent to the cost.*
3. *He works especially late.*
4. *It's especially cold at this time of year.*
5. *In fact most of our customers are in the U.S.*
6. *My Internet connection is particularly slow at this time of day.*
7. *Actually, the system works well.*
8. *We sell this product primarily to Europeans.*
9. *The product sells principally in the U.S.*
10. *In reality, this market is not so profitable.*
11. *I specifically warned them about this.*

Task 6.15

請再聽一次聽力 6.1 中電話會議和聽力 6.4 中面對面會議的錄音，看能聽出多少個特定的 set-phrases。

Task 6.15 ▶參考答案

在這兩個聽力練習中，各位應該能夠從中各聽出一個強調的單字語詞和一個強調的 set-phrases。

在 Unit 3 中，各位已學過如何談論目前案子的未來計畫。如果回到該節再看一次當時所學的語彙（請參見必備語庫 3.2），就會發現其中沒有一個 set-phrase 是含 will 的。然而在剛剛聽到的聽力 6.4 會議錄音當中，各位可能已經注意到東尼說了 I'll do it。在本書這最後的一節中，我們要學的正是一些含 will 的 set-phrases。

在談論案子的現況之時，便可祭出在必備語庫 3.2 中學到的 set-phrases。不過當你自告奮勇表示願意負責某事、提出要求或問題，或追蹤行動計畫時，許多包含 will 的 set-phrases 都能派上用場。而這些 set-phrases 就在後面的必備語庫 6.4 中，讓我們來看一看吧。

Task 6.16

請將 set-phrases 分類，在各個 set-phrase 旁邊寫上所屬的類別字母（如 O、R 和 F）。請參考範例所示。

O = making Offers	R = making Requests or inquiries	F = Following up
F	I'll be in touch.	
	I'll call you later about it.	
	I'll do it.	
	I'll drop you a line.	
	I'll get back to you.	
	I'll get it.	
	I'll give you a ring/call.	
	I'll handle it.	
	I'll look after it.	
	I'll look into it.	
	I'll see what I can do.	
	I'll see you then.	
	I'll send it tomorrow.	
	I'll sort it out.	
	I'll take care of it.	
	I'll V	
	How long will it take?	
	How much will it cost?	
	Shall I do it?	
	Will you do it?	
	Will you help me with this?	
	Will you V?	

Task 6.16 ▶參考答案

請研讀下面的必備語庫 6.4 和解析。

電話和會議 必備語庫 6.4

Making offers

I'll do it.

I'll get it.

I'll handle it.

I'll look after it.

I'll look into it.

I'll see what I can do.

Shall I do it?

I'll V ....

I'll sort it out.

I'll take care of it.

Making requests or inquiries

How long will it take?

How much will it cost?

Will you do it?

Will you help me with this?

Will you V?

Following up

I'll be in touch.

I'll call you later about it.

I'll drop you a line.

I'll get back to you.

I'll give you a ring/call.

I'll see you then.

I'll send it tomorrow.

I'll sort it out.

I'll take care of it.

I'll V ....

語庫解析

- 各位可能會注意到，有的 set-phrases 出現在多個類別當中，這是因為不了解全面狀況的時候，很難說清楚到底這些 set-phrases 是什麼意思。例如，I'll sort it out. 可能是指提供某事或指追蹤某事，甚或是表明自願負責追蹤某事。
- 然而有一個重點各位必須明白和記住的，就是此處所有的 set-phrases 都不是用來描述之前所做的安排或計畫。
- 請注意，此處所有的 set-phrases 提出問題或要求時都是以疑問句的形式。
- 請注意，說 I'll V 的時候應該都要將 I 和 will 縮寫為 I'll。因為 I will 聽起來非常不自然。
- 嚴格來說 shall 和 will 不完全相同，不過常用 Shall I do it？來詢問自己是否該負責某事，所以在此也加以介紹。
- I'll give you a ring. 是 I'll call you. 的意思。

Task **6.17** 聽力 6.6   52

建議各位利用聽力 6.6 練習必備語庫 6.4 set-phrases 的發音。也請再聽一次聽力 6.1 電話會議和聽力 6.4 面對面會議的錄音，看各位是否能夠聽出更多包含 will 的 set-phrases。此外，以當時的情況來說，這些 set-phrases 各是什麼意思？

Task **6.17** ▶參考答案

各位應該聽得出來，在這兩個聽力練習中，三種包含 will 的 set-phrases 各出現一次（即 making offers、making requests or inquiries 和 following up）。如果有聽不清楚的 set-phrases，可翻閱書末所附的對照文。

好，本單元的學習到此結束。在完成本書的學習之前，請回到本單元前面看一看學習目標的清單，以確定所有的學習目標都已達成。

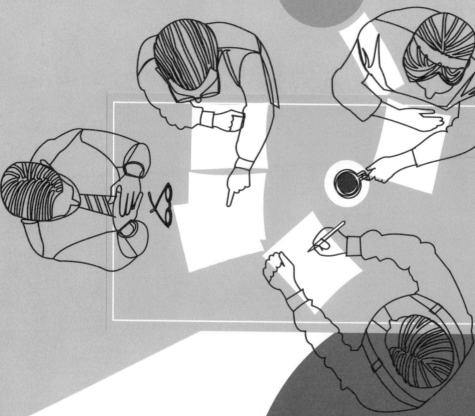

附　錄

Appendices
APPENDICES
Appendices
Appendices
Appendices
APPENDICES
Appendices
Appendices
Appendices

附錄一：電話和會議必備語庫

讀完本書之後，可以繼續使用本附錄，作為準備電話和會議時的參考，或留在手邊以便隨時複習。

必備語庫 1.1 電話應答　　　　　p.51

Making the call 打電話

Is X there please?

Can I speak to X?

Could I speak to X please?

I'd like to speak to X please.

X here.

This is X speaking.

This is X from Y.

Hello, my name's X and I'm calling from Y.

I'll call back later.

I'll hold.

Taking the call 接電話

Can I help you?

Hold on please.

I'll just put you through.

Let me put you through.

I'm afraid he's off sick.

I'm afraid he's on the other line.

I'm afraid he's tied up at the moment.

I'm afraid he's unavailable at the moment.

I'm afraid she's in a meeting.

I'm afraid she's not here just now.

Speaking.

This is X speaking.

X here.

Leaving a message 留話給對方

Can I leave a message?

Could you take a message?

Could you give her a message?

Ready?

Could you read that back to me?

Have you got that?

Taking a message 幫對方留話

Can I take a message?

Would you like to leave a message?

Can I have your name, please?

OK, go ahead please.

Could you repeat that, please?

Let me read that back to you.

Anything else?

必備語庫 2.1 會議展開 I　　　　p.70

Step 1 Signal the beginning 示意會議開始

OK, shall we get going?

OK, shall we start?

You guys ready there?

We're ready here.

Everyone's ready here.

OK, is everyone ready?

We're ready at our end.

The line's ready.

Step 2 Introduce the other team members 介紹小組其他成員

OK, we've got X people here.

Let me just introduce who we've got at our end.

OK, we've got X people at our end.

OK, at our end we've got X and Y.

OK, here we've got X and Y.

Step 4 Check the connection 檢查連線

Can you hear us clearly?

How's your connection?

The line's bad. Let me try again.

Can you hear us OK?

The line's good. Let's go.

必備語庫 2.2 會議展開 II　　p.72

Step 3 Introducing yourself 自我介紹

Hi there, I'm X.

Hello, this is X.

Hi, you can call me X.

Hello, my name is X.

Hello, X here.

必備語庫 2.3 會議展開 III　　p.72

Step 5 State the purpose of the meeting 陳述會議目的

We're having this meeting to V ....

We're having this meeting because + clause.

The purpose of this meeting is to V ....

The reason I've called this meeting is to V ....

The reason I've called this meeting is because + clause.

What we want to do today is V ....

What we need to do today is V ....

What we have to do today is V ....

必備語庫 2.4 處理通訊問題 　　　　p.74

Can you hear us?

Can you say that last bit again please? We didn't get that.

Can you slow down a bit, please?

Can you speak up a bit, please?

Can you turn up your microphone?

Hello?

I think we've lost you.

It's a bad line.

It's a bit hissy.

Let's try again.

Our connection is weak.

Sorry, I didn't catch that last bit.

Sorry, again please.

The line's not very good.

There's a bit of a delay.

There's a problem with the line.

There's an echo.

There's some static.

We can hear you, but I don't think you can hear us.

We can't hear you.

We can't hear you. Can you hear us?

We'll call you.

We're having problems hearing you here.

必備語庫 3.1 平行式簡報的架構　　p.93

Beginning 開始

I'd like to make a few remarks about n.p.

I'd like to update you all on n.p.

I just want to brief you all on n.p.

First, ...

Firstly, ...

To begin, ...

To start with, ...

First of all, ...

Adding 補充說明

Secondly, ...

Thirdly, ...

Second, ...

Third, ...

Also, ...

Another thing ...

As well as this, ...

Then, ...

What's more, ...

And another thing, ...

In addition, ...

Besides that, ...

And on top of that, ...

Not only that, but ...

... plus the fact that + clause.

Moreover, ...

Furthermore, ...

Turning to n.p.

Let's move on to n.p.

Moving on now to n.p.

I would now like to turn briefly to n.p.

The next issue I would like to focus on is n.p.

Illustrating 說明

For example, ...

... i.e., ...

For instance, ...

Take the way that + clause.

Take for example n.p.

To give you an idea, take n.p.

To give you an idea, take the way that + clause.

... such as ...

To give you an idea, look at n.p.

To give you an idea, look at the way that + clause.

Look at the way that + clause.

By way of illustration let's look at n.p.

By way of illustration let's look at the way that + clause.

A case in point is n.p.

... like ...

Contrasting 對比

However, ...

On the one hand, ..., but on the other (hand) ...

In spite of n.p. I still think that + clause.

But then again, ...

Even so, ...

One exception to this is n.p.

必備語庫 3.2 垂直式簡報的進度報告　　　p.100

Describing completed results 描述已達成的結果	Describing uncompleted activities 描述未完成的事項	Describing angements 描述未來的安排
... so that's done.	... so that still needs more work.	Our intention is to V ...
... so that's ready to go.	... so that still needs to be done.	Our plan is to V ...
... so that's finished.	... so that's not ready yet.	We intend to V ...
We've p.p. ...	... we are working on it.	We're (also) going to V ...
We've already p.p. ...	Right now, we're in the middle of Ving ...	We're making arrangements for n.p. ...
We've decided to V ...	We haven't managed to V ... yet.	We're making arrangements to V ...
We've just p.p. ...	We haven't p.p. yet ...	We're taking steps to V ...
We've managed to V ...	We're in the process of Ving ...	We're Ving ...
	We're trying to V ...	We've made arrangements for n.p. ...
	We've been Ving ...	We've made arrangements to V ...
	... we're still trying.	

必備語庫 3.3 處理會議中斷　　　p.106

Interrupting 插話

Sorry.

Sorry to interrupt, but ...

Look, I'm sorry to interrupt, but ...

Can I add something?

Can I add here that + clause?

Can I just point out that + clause?

Excuse me.

Excuse me for interrupting, but ...

I don't mean to interrupt, but ...

May I come in here?

May I interrupt you for a moment?

May I?

I'd like to add something here if I may.

If I could just come in here.

Preventing interruptions 防止插話

Hang on.

Hold on a moment.

Just a moment.

Can I just finish?

If I might just finish.

Please let me finish.

You've interrupted me.

Allowing interruptions 允許插話

Sure.

Yes.

Go ahead.

Oh, please do.

Yes, of course.

Returning to your point 回歸正題

Anyway, ...

Coming back to what I was saying earlier, ...

Going back to what I was saying before, ...

In any case, ...

So, to return to n.p. ...

So, to return to what I was saying, ...

To get back to what I was saying, ...

Well, anyway, as I said before, ...

Well, as I was saying before I was interrupted, ...

Well, ...

What was I saying? Oh yes.

Where was I? Oh yes.

必備語庫 3.4 參閱講義　　　p.109

If you look here, you can see n.p.

If you look at page X, you can see n.p.

If you look there, you can see n.p.

If you look at page X, you can see what I mean.

You can see this on page X.

See page X for more details on this.

Look at page X for more details on this.

Check out page X for more details on this.

Page X shows n.p.

This slide shows n.p.

I've put the details in my report on page X.

You can see my report for more details on this.

Check out my report for more details on this.

You can see that + clause.

You should be able to see that + clause

必備語庫 3.5 概括性說法　　　p.115

...basically...

...for the most part...

...has a tendency to V...

...on the whote...

...roughly speaking...

...tends to V...

...usually...

As a rule, ...

At a rough estimate...

By and large, ...

Generally speaking, ...

In general, ...

In most cases, ...

In my experience, ...

Most of the time, ...

Usually, ...

必備語庫 3.6 語意含糊的說法　　　　　　p.117

Numbers 數字
about X
around X
X-odd
X or so
X-ish
X or something

Words 文字
X or anything
...like...
...sort of...
...kind of...

必備語庫 4.1 ：疑難排解 I　　　　　　p.125

Describing the problem 描述問題
... is giving us problems.
... is giving us trouble.
... doesn't work.
... won't work.
... doesn't work properly/very well/ when(ever) + clause.
... won't work properly/very well/ when(ever) + clause.
It doesn't seem to V ....
It doesn't seem to be Ving ....
It seems that + clause.
It seems to V ....
It seems to have p.p. ....
We can't V ....
We can't seem to V ....
We seem to be Ving ....
We seem to have p.p. ....
We're having problems Ving ....
We're having problems with n.p. ....
We're having trouble Ving ....
We're having trouble with n.p. ....

Asking for help 請求協助
Any advice?
Any suggestions?
How can we ...?
How do we ...?
How do you ...?
How does it ...?
How does X work?
What can we do?
What shall we do?
Can you help?
Please help.
Is it possible to V ...?
Any advice you can give would be greatly appreciated.
Do you have any other ideas about how to solve this?

註：p.p.代表過去分詞

電話和會議 **必備語庫 4.2** ：**疑難排解 II**　　　　p.130

Guessing the cause
猜測原因

... could be because of n.p.

... could be because + clause.

... could be due to n.p.

... could be due to the fact that + clause.

... could be n.p.

... may be because of n.p.

... may be because + clause.

... may be due to n.p.

... may be due to the fact that + clause.

... may be n.p.

... might be because of n.p.

... might be due to n.p.

... might be due to the fact that + clause.

... might be n.p.

... you might have forgotten to V ....

... you may have forgotten to V ....

Suggesting a solution
建議解決方案

Check n.p.

Check that + clause.

Have you remembered to V ...?

Have you tried Ving ...?

Have you p.p. ...?

How about Ving ...?

How about if you V?

Let's V ....

What about Ving ...?

What about if you V ...?

Why don't you V ...?

You could try Ving ....

必備語庫 4.3 提議性說法 p.135

Making a proposal 提出建議方案

Formal 正式

My proposal here is that we V ...

I would like to suggest at this point that we V ...

My recommendation here is that we V ...

I propose that we V ...

So at this point I would like to recommend that we V ...

My suggestion would be to V ...

If I might make a suggestion, I think ...

Informal 非正式

We could V ...

We should V ...

We ought to V ...

I have an idea!

I've got a great idea!

One way would be to V ...

Perhaps we could V ...

Perhaps we should V ...

What about trying to V ...?

What if we + clause

Why don't we try Ving?

Could we V ...?

Why not V ...?

Would it be a good idea if we + clause?

必備語庫 4.4 提議採納或否決 p.138

Accepting 採納

Not bad.
That sounds feasible.
Yes. Good idea.
Yes, I like that one.
Absolutely!
Marvelous!
Brilliant!
Indeed!
That's a great idea!
This proposal has my full support.
I totally agree with this.
I completely agree.
I'm in agreement.

Rejecting 否決

Well, ...
With respect, ...
Frankly, ...
I'm sorry, but ...
I'm not sure about that.
I don't think that would work.
I'm not so sure that would work.
I don't think that's such a good idea at this stage.
I think that would do more harm than good.
To a certain extent I agree with this, but ...
What you're saying/suggesting is just not feasible.
I'm opposed to this proposal.
I'm afraid I can't support this idea.
I can see many problems in adopting this.
That's no good.
That's not going to get us anywhere.
Do you really think that's a good idea?

必備語庫 4.5 建議、提議和推薦 p.143

... suggest (that) you/we V ...

... recommend (that) you/we V ...

... propose (that) you/we V ...

... suggest Ving ...

... recommend Ving ...

... propose Ving ...

必備語庫 4.6 描述後果 p.149

If we do that,	... will V ...
If we V ...,	... may V ...
If we don't V ...,	... might V ...
Unless we V ...,	... could V ...
Should we V ...,	... will probably V ...

... will V ...

... may V ...

... might V ...

... could V ...

... will probably V ...

it will have the effect of Ving ...

it may end up Ving ...

it's likely that + clause.

... be likely to V ...

there's every chance that + clause.

there's a strong possibility of n.p/Ving ...

there is every/no/little likelihood of n.p. ...

there's every chance of n.p. ...

it's possible that + clause.

it's unlikely that + clause.

there's a strong possibility that + clause.

... be unlikely to V ...

there is every/no/little likelihood that + clause.

必備語庫 5.1 陳述觀點　　　　p.155

Asking for opinions 徵詢意見

What do you reckon?

What do you think?

What's your view?

Do you have any ideas about this?

Can you tell me what you think?

Can you tell me your views on n.p.

What's your position on this?

Where do you stand on this?

Can you comment on this?

Giving opinions 提出看法

I reckon + clause.

I think + clause.

In my opinion, ...

In my view, ...

I believe + clause.

I firmly believe + clause.

As I see it, ...

To my mind, ...

My own view is that + clause.

My view is that + clause.

My position is that + clause.

There's no doubt in my mind that + clause.

To my way of thinking, ...

From my point of view, ...

It seems to me that + clause.

As far as I can make out, ...

必備語庫 5.2 贊同與表示異議 p.161

Agreeing 贊同

Me too.

I agree.

Yes, I agree.

Absolutely.

Indeed.

I agree completely.

I think that's right.

I think you're right.

You're absolutely right.

I totally agree with you.

I'm in agreement with X.

I suppose you're right.

I guess you're right.

Disagreeing 表示異議

No, I don't agree.

I disagree entirely.

Yes but, ...

I'm afraid I don't see it like that.

I'm afraid I have to disagree.

I'm afraid I disagree.

I really can't agree with you on that.

Well, I'm not sure.

Well, that's not how I see it at all.

Yes, but don't you think that + clause?

Yes, possibly, but what about ...?

I can see your point, but surely + clause.

I agree up to a point, but + clause.

I agree in principle, but + clause.

必備語庫 5.3 釐清論點 p.165

Asking for clarification
要求釐清

So would I be correct in saying that ...?

When you say ..., do you mean ...?

Correct me if I'm wrong, but ....

So basically what you're saying is ....

Could you go over that last point again, please? I'm afraid I didn't quite catch it.

What do you mean by that?

Can you explain why ...?

Do you mean ...?

So you want us to ....

So you think we should ....

So you're of the opinion that ....

Is that right?

Clarifying
釐清論點

Well, put simply, ...

Basically, what I'm trying to say is ....

That isn't quite what I said.

That isn't quite what I meant.

I'm afraid there seems to have been a slight misunderstanding.

What I mean is ....

Let me put it another way.

What I'm saying here is ....

Don't misunderstand me.

If I said that, I didn't mean to ....

That's not what I said at all.

No, hang on, that's not what I mean.

必備語庫 5.4 委婉説法 p.172

Statements 評語

... would ...

... not (a) very (pos. adj.) noun.

Suggestions 建議

Wouldn't ... be more adj.?

Would ... be more adj.?

Wouldn't ...?

Couldn't ...?

Shouldn't ...?

註：pos. adj.（positive adjective）指肯定形容詞。

必備語庫 5.5 直接説法 p.176

Frankly, ...

To put it bluntly, ...

Well, to be honest, ...

With respect, ...

I'm sorry, but ....

I'm afraid ....

To be quite frank, ...

必備語庫 6.1 人際技巧 p.183

Bringing someone in 加入其他人的支援

At this point I'd like to bring in X.

I think X would like to say something.

Yes, X, please go ahead.

X, do you have something to say at this point?

What are your views, X?

Perhaps X would like to answer that?

At this stage I'd like to call on X to brief us on n.p.

I'd like to invite X to present his/her views.

X, would you like to come in here?

X, would you care to comment?

I'd like to call on X to answer that.

Allocating responsibility 分派責任

Would anyone like to oversee this project?

Can someone volunteer to take this on?

X, could you please be responsible for that?

X, I'd like to ask you to take this on.

X, could you make sure about this?

X, will you be able to handle this?

I'm going to ask X to be responsible for Ving, and Y to V ....

X, can you find out and get back to us?

X, can you be in charge of this, please?

X, I'd like to put you in charge of this.

X, can you take care of this?

必備語庫 6.2 組織架構的技巧 p.188

Summarizing 重述要點

Briefly, ...

In short, ...

To sum up, ...

To summarize, ...

OK, let me just go through the main points again.

Well, if I could just sum up the discussion at this point.

Briefly, the main points that have been made are, ...

If I may just go over the main points raised so far.

Confirming 確認要點

OK, so if I could just confirm our understanding of this.

So, are we all agreed that + clause?

So, can I just check that + clause?

So, can I just confirm that + clause?

So, can I just make sure we are all OK with this?

Is that correct?

Is that right?

Is that OK with you?

Are we all OK with this?

So, are we all agreed that + clause?

Is this clear at your end?

To confirm, I think we are in agreement on n.p.

To confirm, I think we are in agreement on the fact that + clause.

Establishing action points 確立行動計畫

OK, we'll V ....

We'll handle it at our end.

We'll sort that out.

We'll take care of n.p., and you'll take care of n.p.

We'll take the lead here.

X will be in charge of n.p.

Moving on 繼續往下討論

OK, next we need to discuss n.p.

OK, the next question we need to look at is n.p.

OK, that's that. Now, moving on, ...

OK, I'd like to move on to the next point on the agenda now.

Let's move on, can we?

Any other points on that? OK, let's turn to the next item.

Can we move on to the next point, please?

At this stage I think we need to move on to the next item on the agenda.

Can we move on to the next point, please?

Does anyone else have anything to say on this before we move on?

必備語庫 6.3 強調特定看法 p.194

... actually ...

... especially ...

... particularly ...

... primarily ...

... principally ...

... specifically ...

The fact of the matter is that + clause.

The truth of the matter is that + clause.

In fact, ...

Actually, ...

In reality, ...

In particular, ...

必備語庫 6.4 含 will 的 set-phrases

Making offers 提出貢獻

I'll do it.

I'll get it.

I'll handle it.

I'll look after it.

I'll look into it.

I'll see what I can do.

Shall I do it?

I'll V ....

I'll sort it out.

I'll take care of it.

Making requests or inquiries 請求或詢問

How long will it take?

How much will it cost?

Will you do it?

Will you help me with this?

Will you V?

Following up 後續追蹤

I'll be in touch.

I'll call you later about it.

I'll drop you a line.

I'll get back to you.

I'll give you a ring/call.

I'll see you then.

I'll send it tomorrow.

I'll sort it out.

I'll take care of it.

I'll V ....

附錄二：聽力練習對照文

　　本附錄僅包括電話或會議聽力練習的錄音稿，供各位參考對照。至於語庫部分的發音練習，則可參見附錄一的電話和會議必備語庫。

Unit 1

Listening 1.1　　　　 03

M:	Bell Computers Limited, can I help you?
Mary:	Hello, I'd like to speak to Mike please.
M:	Hold on please.
M:	Hello, I'm afraid Mike's unavailable right now. He's in a meeting. Can I take a message?
Mary:	Yes, can you please let him know I called and ask him to call me back as soon as he can? My name's Mary, and I'm calling from Happy Travel. My number is 123 456 789.
M:	Sorry, could you repeat that please?
Mary:	Yes, 123 456 789, Mary from Happy Travel. Have you got that?
M:	Let me read that back to you: 123 456 789, Mary from Happy Travel. I'll ask him to get back to you as soon as he can.
Mary:	Great. Thanks.
M:	Anything else?
Mary:	No, that's it. Thanks. Bye
M:	Bye.

Listening 1.2

 04

W:	Hello, Happy Travel
Mike:	Hello, is Mary there please?
W:	Umm, I can't see her. Let me see if she's in the other office.
Mike:	OK, I'll hold.
W:	Hello?
Mike:	Hello.
W:	She's in the other office. Let me put you through.
Mary:	Hello.
Mike:	Hello? Mary?
Mary:	Speaking.
Mike:	This is Mike from Bell Computers.
Mary:	Oh, yes, thanks for getting back to me.
Mike:	That's OK. I tried to call you earlier but I couldn't get through to you.

Unit 2

Listening 2.1 08

Leader A:	OK, I think we're ready at our end.
Leader B:	Yes, everyone's ready here. Can you let us know who you've got there?
Leader A:	OK, at our end we've got Laurence from the technical support department, and Cindy from the design team, and I'm Jude.
Laurence:	Hi there, I'm Laurence.
Cindy:	Hello, this is Cindy.
Leader B:	OK, we've got just two people at our end. Myself — my name's Candy — and Tony, the project technician.
Tony:	Hello, everyone, Tony here.
Leader A:	Can you hear us clearly?
Leader B:	Yes, the line's good. Let's go.
Leader A:	OK, we're having this meeting because you've discovered some technical problems with the work we've sent you so far. Could you begin by describing exactly what the technical problems are?

Listening 2.5

 12

Team B:	... so I think what we need to do is (XXXXXXXXXX) finish on time.
Team A:	Sorry, Tom, can you say that last bit again please? We didn't get that.
Team B:	Oh, OK, I said (XXXXXXXXXX) on time.
Team A:	Sorry Tom, We're having problems hearing you here. It's a bit hissy. Can you hear us?
Team B:	(XXXXXXXXXX)
Team A:	Hello?
Team B:	(XXXXXXXXXX) but I don't think you can hear us. (XXXXXXXXXX) Hello? (XXXXXXXXXX)
Team A:	Tom, if you can hear me, I think we've lost you. There's a problem with the line. Let's try again. We'll call you.
Team B:	(XXXXXXXXXX) OK (XXXXXXXXXX).

Listening 2.7 14

Leader A:	You guys ready there?
Leader B:	Um, just a minute, we're just waiting for Eduardo. Oh here he is, right, yes, we're ready at our end.
Leader A:	OK, we've got three people on our side: Jennifer from sales, and Jack from marketing, and I'm Nancy.
Jennifer:	Hello, I'm Jennifer.
Jack:	Hi, you can call me Jack.
Leader B:	OK, let me just introduce who we've got at our end. There's myself — my name's Jason — and Eduardo, the country buyer.
Eduardo:	Hi there, I'm Eduardo.
Leader A:	How's your connection?
Leader B:	Yes, the line's good. Let's go.
Leader A:	OK. The purpose of this meeting is to discuss the new lines for next season. It seems that your buyer is not happy with our new line of underwear. Can you tell us why?
Eduardo:	Yes, it's not good enough because (XXXXXXXXX).
Leader A:	Sorry, Eduardo, can you turn up your microphone?
Eduardo:	Like this?
Leader A:	That's better. Can you say that last bit again please? We didn't get that.
Eduardo:	Yes, it makes the women look fat. We tried the knickers on several models and they all look fat. I think it will be difficult to sell. No one wants to look fat in their knickers, you know?
Jack:	Mmm, that's strange. Have you tried using slimmer models?
Eduardo:	Of course, you stupid (XXXXXXXXXX).
Jack:	Sorry, Eduardo. I didn't catch that last bit.

Unit 3

Leader A:	At this point I'd like to ask Tracy from our team to brief you on the results of the research we've conducted into the market.
Leader B:	OK sounds good. Hi Tracy.
Tracy:	Hi there. Can you all hear me clearly?
Team B:	Yes/Sure/It's OK.
Tracy:	OK, well, I'd like to update you all on the ready-to-drink market here in Taiwan. First, let's look at the character of the market. As a rule, the main outlet for this kind of product is convenience stores such as 7-Eleven and Niko Mart. Supermarkets also usually carry quite a large range of these products. However, the main bulk of sales come from convenience stores. If you've been to Taiwan, you'll know how many convenience stores there are here, around three on every corner.
Leader B:	Tracy, may I interrupt you for a moment?
Tracy:	Sure.
Leader B:	Can you give us some specific figures on the size of those two channels, supermarkets and convenience stores?
Tracy:	Yes, if you look at page four of the handouts I sent you, you'll see those figures there. Can you see?
Leader B:	Oh, yes, right, very good.
Tracy:	Let's move on to look at what kind of products are the most popular. Page five shows the range of products and their market share. You can see that bottled teas tend to be bigger sellers compared with coffee, sports drinks, soft drinks, and beer. Moreover, the market has been kind of growing for the last two years with more local products coming onto the market. This means that the market is getting more competitive. I'd like....
Leader B:	Tracy, this is John here. Sorry to interrupt, but can you tell us whether the local products are luxury items or not?

Tracy:	Hang on. I'm just coming to that. Most of the tea products on the market are not luxury items, and what's more, most of them are not milk tea products.
Leader A:	OK, thanks Tracy. Any questions? No? OK, now I'd like to ask Mike to talk us through what's happening with the consumer survey.
Mike:	Hi everybody. OK, so far we've already commissioned the research house to set up focus groups with three different target consumers — young women, young men, and high school kids — and the materials for the focus sessions are complete, so that's done. Right now we're in the middle of getting more information about the spending habits of these groups and we're also in the process of building a profile of the target consumer. We haven't managed to identify any other possible target market segments, but we're working on it. We're making arrangements to commission this research from another research house to spread the work a bit.
Team B:	Can I just point out that we must have a target profile as soon as possible so that we can start to build a marketing campaign for that target?
Mike:	That's right. We'll have it ready very soon. What was I saying? Oh yes, we intend to have the target profile ready by next week at the latest.

Listening 3.8 23

Doris:	OK, I just want to brief you all on the travel market in Taiwan. To start with, generally speaking, the travel industry in Taiwan focuses mainly on tours. This segment of the industry is well developed.
Barry:	Sorry to interrupt, Doris, but can you tell me more about these tour groups, what kind of things they enjoy, and so on?
Doris:	Yes, of course. Most of the time, when Taiwanese travel, they prefer to do so in large groups accompanied by a guide, who usually takes care of everything, for instance, choosing the restaurants, the itinerary, the mode of transport, and things like that. Another thing is that most travelers to the UK tend to be middle aged, around 40 to 50 or so. This age group is less adventurous; they like good hotels, and have money to spend. They kind of prefer to stay in the cities where they feel safer. They are not into mountain climbing in Wales or anything.
Barry:	I don't mean to interrupt, but can you tell me what plans you have for growing the youth market?
Doris:	Just a moment. I'll tell you about that in a minute. Where was I? Oh yes. By way of illustration, let's look at the top five destinations in the UK for this kind of traveler over the last five years. If you look at page ten you can see what I mean. In spite of these characteristics of the market, I still think there is room for growth in the youth sector.
Barry:	So how do you intend to do that?
Doris:	OK, let me tell you what we've been doing. We've been in touch with the Wales and Scottish Tourist development offices here in Taiwan and they're interested in working with us to promote their regions to the youth segment. We've decided to implement an advertising campaign focusing on the excitement of the activities in those regions.
Barry:	May I interrupt you for a moment?
Doris:	Go ahead.
Barry:	How much is it going to cost, and who is going to pay?

Doris: Well, at the moment we are trying to work out those details. We haven't managed to come up with a concrete plan yet, but we are working on it.

Barry: I see. OK. So what's next?

Doris: Well, our intention is to have some features about these regions in some youth magazines. We're also going to run some ads on TV and put some flyers in places where young people go, like the gym and student organizations. We're making arrangements to have some activities at big shopping malls and department stores around town.

Unit 4

Listening 4.1 26

Team A:	Well, we seem to be having problems with heat control. The whole unit gets too hot very quickly, and melts the cable to the fan, which then stops working. It seems that the fan cable is too close to the power source. Is it possible to redesign that area of the motherboard? Or do you have any other ideas about how to solve this?
Team B1:	Hmm, that's a tricky one, isn't it. Based on our experience, it might be a malfunction in the current converter. We've had problems with other models.
Team B2:	On the other hand, it could be due to the fact that the original design of the motherboard has some limitations.
Team B1:	Well, what about if we try two things? Let's use a different current converter and see if the problem still persists. If it does, we'll go back to the motherboard and see if we can redesign that bit, as you suggested.
Team B2:	Does that sound like a good idea?
Team A:	Yes, we're happy with that. How long will it take?
Team B2:	Tony?
Team B1:	I'll see what I can do. I think we can find the result with the changed converter in a couple of days. I'll get back to you by the end of the week.
Team B2:	By the end of the week. Is that OK with you?
Team A:	Fine. OK, next we need to discuss the SR 3200.

Listening 4.6

A: OK, we've heard from Morris about the situation. The choices facing us are to go ahead with the launch of the TomK brand and risk losing this very valuable customer, or to drop the whole idea of launching an own-brand product and focus on ODM production, as we always have. I'd like to hear your ideas on this now. Julie, what do you think?

Julie: Well, if I might make a suggestion, I propose that we stick to our plans and continue with the launch of the TomK brand. We've invested too much to walk away from it. So at this point I would like to recommend that we announce our own brand to all our ODM customers.

A: Mmm. James?

James: I'm opposed to this proposal. I think that would do more harm than good. At the moment most of our revenue comes from ODM and OEM. We don't know what kind of revenue our own brand will generate. It's basically a gamble. If it doesn't work and we can't sell any of our own-brand products because there's no market recognition, and at the same time we lose all our ODM customers, we'll be out of business in two months. My recommendation here is that we drop the TomK brand and focus on our core business, aiming to be market leader.

A: Mmm. Joan?

Joan: Yes, good idea. This proposal has my full support. I've been against TomK brand from the start. Expenses are too high.

A: Mmm. Jackie?

Jackie: I have an idea. Would it be a good idea if we delayed the launch of TomK brand for one year, produced our customer's products, and see what problems they have with it. Then we could, you know, how can I say this, "borrow" some of their ideas to make improvements to our own-brand products. What if we launch a better version of our own-brand products in a couple of months, say after six months? That way, we can get to keep this big order, make improvements to our own-brand products without spending lots of our own money on testing and quality control, and still launch the brand, only later?

All: Absolutely! / Marvelous! / Brilliant! / Indeed! / I completely agree.

Unit 5

A-Max:	So you want the system to work like this: The name goes in the first input field, the next column is the date of the previous visit, and the third column is the room type.
B-Mary:	Yes, that sounds right.
B-Tony:	Do you mean the room for the previous visit or this visit?
A-Max:	Oh. Good point. Umm. What I mean is the previous visit.
B-Tony:	OK, I think we should add two more fields after the name. One field for the address of the customer, in case there are customers with the same names, and the other field for the agent booking number from the previous visit. In my view this information should go before the room type column.
A-Max:	Oh, OK. Mary? What do you reckon?
B-Mary:	Hmm. Well, that's not how I see it at all. You see, from my point of view, the room information is more important than the address and booking number.
B-Tony:	I'm afraid I disagree. For the finance department, and the marketing department as well, it's important to know the agent booking number so that we can control the room prices and bookings more efficiently.
B-Mary:	Yes, but the other information is more important for the house management team and front office.
B-Tony:	But the front office wouldn't be using this field at this stage of the process. This is the pre-stay process.
A-Max:	So basically, Tony, what you're saying is that we need the system for the back office not front office. Is that right?
B-Tony:	No, hang on, that's not what I mean. We need the system for both front and back office, but at this stage of the process, the back office is going to be the main user. Mary thinks it should be front office users only.
B-Mary:	No, what I'm saying here is that I think the front office will probably be the main user at this stage of the process. Max, do you have any ideas about this?

A-Max:	Well, to be honest, I'm in agreement with Tony. At this stage, isn't it more likely to be the back office people using the system? If so, wouldn't it be more efficient to prioritize that kind of information first?
B-Mary:	OK, I suppose you're right.

Listening 5.9

Joyce:	So my suggestion here is that we hold off with the project until we get more details from the client. Mike, what do you think?
Mike:	As I see it, we don't have any alternative. We can't go ahead because the specs we've got don't match. We need clarification before we can proceed.
Joyce:	I think you're right. Julian, what's your view?
Julian:	Well, I'm not sure. I know there's a problem with the specs, but to my mind there are still other things we can work on until we get clarification.
Joyce:	What do you mean by that?
Julian:	Well, put simply, we can still prepare samples for the client, show them the color, and the materials. In any case, we don't want to delay the project if we can help it, because a delay is going to cost us, not the client.
Tracy:	I agree completely. I would prefer to continue with the project. I don't think we should hold off the whole thing just because the specs are not clear. To put it bluntly, we can clear them up in thirty minutes with a phone call.
Mike:	So you want us to carry on and ignore the problem with the specs? To be quite frank, I think we're making a mistake if we think the specs are not important.
Tracy:	I'm afraid there seems to have been a slight misunderstanding. Of course I think the specs are important, but they don't need to hold everything else up. I can call the chief engineer at the client side this afternoon and get clarification on the specs.
Mike:	Well, I think we should wait until we clear up the problems with the specs.
Julian:	I'm afraid I have to disagree, Mike. Couldn't we still get on with the marketing plan for the project? The specs aren't going to change that much, and any marketing plan we come up with is not going to change that much if the specs change, right?

Unit 6

Listening 6.1 47

Team A:	OK, let me just go through the main points again. The specs you've been sent do not conform to EU safety guidelines and will need to be redesigned. Is that right?
Team B:	That's correct.
Team A:	OK, oh, hang on. I think Cindy would like to say something.
Cindy:	Yes, could you send us your version of the guidelines so that we can be sure we're working to the same set? Because the fact of the matter is that there are actually often a few different versions.
Team A:	Good idea. Julie?
Team B:	No problem, we'll sort that out and send you the guidelines this afternoon.
Team A:	OK, we'll spend some time studying the guidelines and then come up with new specs, probably towards the middle of next month. Cindy, can you be in charge of this please?
Cindy:	OK. I'll get back to you.
Team A:	Cindy will be in charge of this and will contact you. Any other points on that? OK, let's turn to the next item.

Listening 6.4 50

Mary:	OK. Briefly, the main points that have been made are that most people think the reason for the low product performance is that the product doesn't taste good, and that our competitor's products are healthier. We need to make some modifications to the taste and add some healthier ingredients. Are we all OK with this?
Others:	That's correct. / Yes. / Sounds good.
Mary:	Just a minute. Morris, do you have something to say at this point?
Morris:	Yes, it's just occurred to me that there might be other reasons why the product didn't perform so well, particularly the pricing strategy. Perhaps people think it's too cheap. What about positioning it as a luxury product? In fact, that might be cheaper than modifying the ingredients and taste.
Others:	Good idea. / Why don't we try that? / Sounds good to me.
Mary:	OK, we'll try two things. Let's reposition the brand with new marketing and a new name. Morris, I'd like to put you in charge of this.
Morris:	Sure.
Mary:	Secondly, let's keep the branding that we've got and modify the product. Would anyone like to oversee this?
Tony:	I'll do it.
Mary:	Great. We'll meet again in one month to try the new product and to see the new marketing strategy. OK, at this stage I think we need to move on to the next point on the agenda.

附錄三：學習目標記錄表

各位可利用這張表來設立學習目標和記錄學習狀況，以找出改進之道。

第一欄：寫下你在接下來一週內預定學習或使用的 set-phrases。
第二欄：寫下你在當週實際使用該 set-phrases 的次數。
第三欄：寫下你使用該 set-phrases 時遇到的困難或該注意的事項。

預計使用的 set-phrases	使用次數	附註

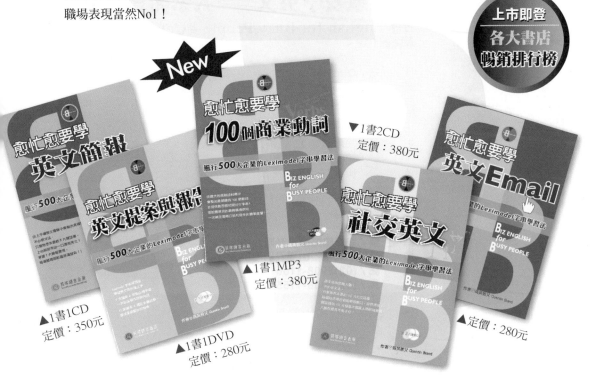

國家圖書館出版品預行編目資料

愈忙愈要學英文：大家開會說英文 ＝ Biz English for
Busy People: Conferences and Meetings / Quentin
Brand作；金振寧譯.
－－初版. －－臺北市；貝塔，2007〔民96〕
　面： 　　公分

ISBN 978-957-729-624-5（平裝附光碟片）

1. 商業英文－會話

805.188　　　　　　　　　　　　　　95024554

愈忙愈要學英文──大家開會說英文
Biz English for Busy People—Conferences and Meetings

作　　者 / Quentin Brand
譯　　者 / 金振寧
執行編輯 / 胡元媛

出　　版 / 貝塔出版有限公司
地　　址 / 台北市100館前路12號11樓
電　　話 / (02)2314-2525
傳　　真 / (02)2312-3535
郵　　撥 / 19493777貝塔出版有限公司
客服專線 / (02)2314-3535
客服信箱 / btservice@betamedia.com.tw

總 經 銷 / 時報文化出版企業股份有限公司
地　　址 / 桃園縣龜山鄉萬壽路二段 351 號
電　　話 / (02) 2306-6842

出版日期 / 2007年1月初版一刷
定　　價 / 350元
ISBN：978-957-729-624-5

Biz English for Busy People—Conferences and Meetings
Copyright 2007 by Quentin Brand
Published by Beta Multimedia Publishing

喚醒你的英文語感！

對折後釘好，直接寄回即可！

100 台北市中正區館前路12號11樓

 貝塔語言出版 收
Beta Multimedia Publishing

寄件者住址 □□□

貝塔語言出版
Beta Multimedia Publishing

讀者服務專線（02）2314-3535　　讀者服務傳真（02）2312-353
客戶服務信箱 btservice@betamedia.com.tw

www.betamedia.com.tw

謝謝您購買本書！！

貝塔語言擁有最優良之英文學習書籍，為提供您最佳的英語學習資訊，您可填妥此表後寄回（免貼郵票）將可不定期收到本公司最新發行書訊及活動訊息！

姓名：＿＿＿＿＿＿＿＿＿＿＿　性別：□男 □女　生日：＿＿＿年＿＿＿月＿＿＿日

電話：(公)＿＿＿＿＿＿＿＿(宅)＿＿＿＿＿＿＿＿(手機)＿＿＿＿＿＿＿＿

電子信箱：＿＿＿＿＿＿＿＿＿＿＿＿＿＿＿＿＿

學歷：□高中職含以下 □專科 □大學 □研究所含以上

職業：□金融 □服務 □傳播 □製造 □資訊 □軍公教 □出版
　　　□自由 □教育 □學生 □其他

職級：□企業負責人 □高階主管 □中階主管 □職員 □專業人士

1. 您購買的書籍是？＿＿＿＿＿＿＿＿＿＿＿＿＿＿＿＿

2. 您從何處得知本產品？(可複選)
　　□書店 □網路 □書展 □校園活動 □廣告信函 □他人推薦 □新聞報導 □其他

3. 您覺得本產品價格：
　　□偏高 □合理 □偏低

4. 請問目前您每週花了多少時間學英語？
　　□ 不到十分鐘 □ 十分鐘以上，但不到半小時 □ 半小時以上，但不到一小時
　　□ 一小時以上，但不到兩小時 □ 兩個小時以上 □ 不一定

5. 通常在選擇語言學習書時，哪些因素是您會考慮的？
　　□ 封面 □ 內容、實用性 □ 品牌 □ 媒體、朋友推薦 □ 價格 □ 其他＿＿＿＿

6. 市面上您最需要的語言書種類為？
　　□ 聽力 □ 閱讀 □ 文法 □ 口說 □ 寫作 □ 其他＿＿＿＿＿

7. 通常您會透過何種方式選購語言學習書籍？
　　□ 書店門市 □ 網路書店 □ 郵購 □ 直接找出版社 □ 學校或公司團購
　　□ 其他＿＿＿＿＿＿

8. 給我們的建議：＿＿＿＿＿＿＿＿＿＿＿＿＿＿＿
＿＿＿＿＿＿＿＿＿＿＿＿＿＿＿＿＿＿＿

喚醒你的英文語感！

Get a Feel for English !